A *Love* for *Tomorrow*

Vanessa MILLER

a novel

WHITAKER
HOUSE

A LOVE FOR TOMORROW
Book Two in the Second Chance at Love Series

Vanessa Miller
www.vanessamiller.com

ISBN: 978-1-60374-208-5
Printed in the United States of America
© 2010 by Vanessa Miller

Whitaker House
1030 Hunt Valley Circle
New Kensington, PA 15068
www.whitakerhouse.com

Library of Congress Cataloging-in-Publication Data
Miller, Vanessa.
  A love for tomorrow / by Vanessa Miller.
    p. cm. — (Second chance at love; bk. 2)
  Summary: "Christian television show host Serenity Williams is determined never to fall in love with another ego-driven pastor, but then she meets Pastor Phillip McKnight, whose kingdom vision and humble personality begin to change her mind"—Provided by publisher.
  ISBN 978-1-60374-208-5 (trade pbk.)
  1. African American churches—Fiction. I. Title.
  PS3613.I5623L68 2010
  813'.6—dc22
                                    2010017486

1 2 3 4 5 6 7 8 9 10   **W**   16 15 14 13 12 11 10

Acknowledgments

I enjoyed every minute of writing *A Love for Tomorrow*. I fell in love with the main characters, Serenity and Phillip, immediately. I knew both characters were more complicated than they first let on. There was something brewing on the inside that would have to come out in order for these characters to be all they could be to each other. So, I just wanted to thank Serenity and Phillip for helping me to discover their layers and peel them back so that the readers could truly get to know them.

I also must thank my agent, Natasha Kern, for all that she does to keep my career on the right track. Christine Whitaker, Cathy Hickling, and Courtney Hartzel of Whitaker House have each worked so hard to help make this series a success that I simply must thank them. You three have been wonderful to me. There are also countless others at Whitaker House whom I have never spoken to but who have nonetheless worked just as hard as the rest of us to make *A Love for Tomorrow* a success, and so I would like to thank the graphics, marketing, and sales departments. I hope to meet all of you soon, but until then, know that I am grateful for the things you do.

And a special thank-you to all of my readers who anxiously await my next book. I couldn't do this with out you. I sure hope you keep reading my books.

Happy reading,
Vanessa

5

Dedication

This book is dedicated to anyone who has ever run from the call of God on his or her life. It's never too late to turn back and do God's will. Keep the faith.

Prologue

"OUR WEDDING IS NEXT WEEK, MICHAEL. HOW CAN you possibly have cold feet now?" Serenity Williams asked her fiancé with her hands on her hips.

"This isn't about cold feet, Serenity. You're not listening to me. I'm telling you, I can't marry you. I've been trying to convince myself for weeks that it will work, but I realize now that it won't."

This was not happening to her. This was some crazy dream that she was going to wake up from any minute, because there was no way that the good reverend, Dr. Michael Randolph—the man she loved and had been planning to marry for the past three years—could be standing in front of her one week before the wedding, trying to call it off. But, just in case this wasn't a dream, Serenity decided to play along. "Okay, Michael. Please tell me exactly what I haven't been listening to."

Michael took off his black fedora, revealing his full head of wavy, black hair. "Can you sit down on the couch with me so we can talk?"

She didn't want to sit down and talk; she wanted to get married. Michael owed her a wedding. After all, she had spent five years with this man. They had dated for two years and then gotten engaged. That had been three years ago. She had told her friends that she and Michael had decided to wait until his ministry got off the ground before getting married, but, in truth, it had been Michael's decision to wait. Now that his ministry was growing, what did he want her to do—wait another five years so he could work on expanding his church so that it reached megachurch status?

Michael sat down on the couch and held out his hand, gesturing for Serenity to join him.

She sat down next to him but said nothing.

"Serenity, the first thing you need to understand is that I love you more than life itself. It is because of how much I love you that I can't go through with this marriage."

When am I going to wake up? Serenity held up her hand. "Wait a minute, now. I'm totally confused. Are you really telling me that you can't marry me because you love me too much?"

"Let me finish, honey," Michael said. He took a deep breath and then trod on. "We've put off our wedding for three years now, because I've been hoping you'll get over your competitive ways. It's this constant rivalry between us that's driving me crazy. I'm afraid that the love I have for you will fade because of the competitive spirit you have."

"The competitive spirit *I* have?" Serenity exploded as she stood up. "I'm not in competition with anybody. I'm just doing what God has called me to do."

"That's what you tell people. But it's obvious that you are competitive. You wouldn't be where you are today if you weren't."

"Okay, so what if I am a little competitive? What does that have to do with you and me? You're the pastor of a church. I don't have a church; I travel all over the world preaching, and I have a television ministry."

"See? That's what I mean," he said, pointing at her. Then, he stood up, too. "You're always throwing the fact that you have a TV ministry in my face. And you love it when other preachers invite you to speak at their churches. You've even been trying to get behind my pulpit for the past year."

"That is not true. I have never asked to preach at your church. I have more speaking engagements than I can accept in a year, so I certainly don't need to beg anybody for the opportunity to preach."

"See, there you go again. Every time you open your mouth, it's always to say something about what you're doing in ministry and how you're in such high demand."

It wasn't true. Serenity had never bragged about her ministry. At least, not in the way Michael was making it sound like she did. Yes, she was grateful that God had allowed her ministry to grow in the manner in which it had over the last two years. And, yes, she expressed that gratitude to anyone who would listen. But she wasn't bragging. She was trying to communicate to others that she understood how blessed she was. Serenity's father was a bishop who presided over seven megachurches and ten smaller to medium-sized ones. He had often tried to get her to take over one of his churches as a pastor, but she didn't believe that God was leading her in that direction.

She had stepped out in faith when she'd started her television ministry on a newly developed cable channel. Her television program was part Oprah, part Joyce Meyer in style. She interviewed many pastors and teachers of the gospel. And then, when she was invited to minister, she brought along her camera crew and broadcast those events on her program, as well. She and Michael had discussed the format of her show at its inception. At the time, he had thought it was a great idea. He'd even told her that he could see her show going big time.

He just hadn't told her that, when it did, he would hold it against her. "Michael, please don't do this. Maybe we need to see a marriage counselor so we can work this out before the wedding."

"Don't you find the fact that we need a marriage counselor before we even get married a bit ludicrous?"

"I don't know about that. What definitely seems ludicrous to me is the fact that you're jealous of a ministry that God's hand is on." She took a deep breath, tried to calm herself, and said, "Look, Michael. I'm thirty-four years old. You're forty-two. We both agreed that now is the perfect time for us to have children. I've waited for you for five years. Why are you backing out now?"

"I'm sorry, Serenity. I just can't marry someone whose ministry overshadows my own. The next thing I know, people will be calling me 'Mr. Williams' instead of 'Pastor Randolph.'" He shook his head. "I just can't deal with that."

This was real—Michael was calling off their wedding—and Serenity felt as if her world was coming to an end. "What do you want me to do, Michael? Do you want me to give up my TV ministry? Is that it?"

He put his hat back on. "No. That won't work. You've created such a following now that, even if you weren't on TV, preachers would still be calling for you to speak at their conferences."

"I don't understand. I thought you loved me."

Michael didn't respond. He picked up his car keys and walked out of the house without looking back.

If he had turned around, he would have seen the tears that flowed down Serenity's face and the longing that she felt way down deep in her heart. But Michael didn't care about that. He cared only about being "overshadowed." Why hadn't she seen this coming? Her best friend, Melinda Marks, had tried to warn her two years ago, when she'd said, "Trying to do the will of God and the will of your man gets hard sometimes."

At the time, Serenity had thought that Melinda was referring to her relationship with Bishop Steven Marks. Steven and Melinda had been engaged long ago, but Steven had felt that he couldn't marry a woman who wanted to preach the gospel rather than stay at home and be a wife and mother. So, he'd called off their wedding. But God's will had prevailed in that situation, and Steven and Melinda had finally gotten married eighteen months ago.

As she wiped the tears from her eyes, Serenity told herself not to worry. Michael would come to his senses, and they would be married on Saturday, as planned.

But on Thursday, her father, Bishop Lawrence Williams, called and informed her that Michael's secretary was phoning everyone on the guest list and letting them know that the wedding had been cancelled. That's when Serenity finally faced the fact that Michael wasn't coming back. He had allowed his ego to override their love, and she was crushed.

"Why didn't you tell me, sweetheart?" her father asked.

"I thought he would change his mind. I just didn't believe he was serious."

Serenity had been calling Michael for the past three days, leaving messages on his answering machine and voice mail, letting him know that she still loved him, and that she still wanted to go through with the wedding. Why should she have to wait ten years for Michael to come to his senses, as Melinda had done with Steven? Serenity was convinced that if they just went ahead and got married, they would be able to work everything out later.

"Why is he doing this?" her father asked, cutting in on her thoughts.

"He says I'm too competitive—that he can't marry a woman who overshadows him and his ministry."

"Oh, sweetheart, I'm so sorry to hear that. But if that's the way he feels, then he doesn't deserve you. I believe that, if you're meant to marry a preacher, God will send one who can handle your anointing."

Serenity didn't respond to her father's remark, and they brought their conversation to an end. But, by the time she had hung up the phone, she had made a very clear resolution. She wouldn't waste another minute of her life on another ego-driven preacher.

ॐ

Pastor Phillip McKnight was a man who had been greatly blessed by God. There was no other explanation for the extraordinary life he'd led. He'd played sixteen years of professional football, being traded only twice and winning a Super Bowl championship with both teams. The last team he'd played for had been the Tampa Bay Buccaneers. He'd been thirty-seven and still fit enough to play, if he'd wanted, when he'd voluntarily retired. But Phillip had other things on his mind. He'd earned millions of dollars from his winning football career, and now he wanted to live out the rest of his life serving God and winning souls for the kingdom.

When he arrived at the new building of the church he pastored, New Destiny, he entered, eager to check on the progress of the construction workers. He had given up a lot to build this church, but he had no regrets. In his lifetime, he had experienced fame and fortune, the likes of which most people only dream about. But none of the things he had accomplished ever truly fulfilled him. Then, one day, he'd met Jesus, and it was as if the blinders came off. He began to see things so much more clearly. He received new direction for his life.

Jimmy Dayton, the foreman for the construction company, met Phillip in the fellowship hall. "I've got something to show you," he told him excitedly.

"Lead the way," Phillip said, hoping that at least one of the rooms in the church was finally finished. They had been making plans for the building for a year and a half, but construction hadn't started until nine months ago. Right now, New Destiny was holding its services in a high school gymnasium, and he was getting ready to come home.

Jimmy opened the double doors to the sanctuary, and Phillip walked in, his eyes beholding the beauty of the navy blue wall-to-wall carpet and the matching cushioned pews, which spanned the three-thousand-seat sanctuary. The glass podium he'd ordered was in the pulpit area, waiting for him to stand behind it and preach the Word. He turned to Jimmy. "This looks incredible! What else is finished?"

"Just your office, but the structure is solid enough for your congregation to have services here soon."

"This is the best news I've had all week!" Phillip exclaimed. "I'm glad I stopped by today. How soon can we start holding our services in here?" He couldn't keep the excitement out of his voice.

"Probably in about two weeks or so," Jimmy said. "We need to get a couple more things done before the safety inspection."

"Okay—but hurry up! I can't wait to have our services in this sanctuary," Phillip said before heading for his new office, where he sat down behind the desk. He finally felt like they were making progress. That sense of satisfaction enabled him to take out the envelope he'd been carrying around all day in his pocket and put it on his desk. He looked at the envelope for a full ten minutes before picking it up and opening it.

Slowly, he unfolded the divorce decree and stared at it for a few moments before throwing it back on his desk. Then, he leaned back in his chair, closed his eyes, and prayed for strength.

One

N O, *THIS MAN IS NOT KEEPING ME WAITING LIKE this*, Serenity thought as she looked at her diamond-studded Gucci watch. It was one of her favorite accessories. The watch had been priced at two grand, but Serenity had talked the store manager into halving the price. Her father always told her that a woman should treat herself to something special every now and then. So, while she'd been on her honeymoon in the Bahamas—without the groom—she'd purchased this gorgeous watch without a second thought. She loved the look and feel of Gucci on her wrist.

But her beautiful timepiece was telling her that her interviewee was twenty minutes late. The infamous Pastor Phillip McKnight had cancelled the interview they'd scheduled for two weeks ago so that he and a group of evangelists, ministers, and church members could travel to Port-au-Prince, Haiti, to help with the disaster relief efforts after the terrible earthquake that had racked the country and claimed so many lives. Serenity wholeheartedly understood Pastor McKnight's desire to be in Haiti during the country's time of need. She had even set up a disaster relief fund on her own Web site, encouraging the viewers of her Christian television show, *Walk This Way*, to donate money. But Pastor McKnight had been back in the States for three days now. What in the world could have caused him to be late for their rescheduled meeting?

Serenity hadn't wanted to interview Pastor McKnight in the first place. She was more comfortable with female preachers and teachers on her show, and she thought that her viewership, consisting predominantly of young to middle-aged women, would benefit most from hearing about the accomplishments and visions of other women around their age. But her producer kept telling her that women were also interested in men who served the Lord. So, here she was, being mistreated by another arrogant pastor who thought the world revolved around his inflated head.

Well, enough was enough. Serenity would not wait a second longer. She was going to gather up her camera crew and head back to Chicago. But, as she stood up, the office door opened, and a broad-shouldered man with skin the color of milk chocolate rushed through it. She had seen Pastor McKnight on television when he'd played for Tampa, but that football helmet must have blocked her view, because she had never imagined that the man was this fine in the flesh. Serenity sat back down and tried to process everything she knew about Pastor Phillip McKnight. He was a former football player who'd started building the church he now pastored a year before retiring from the NFL. She also knew that he was divorced.

"Sorry I'm so late," he said with an apologetic smile. "I got a flat tire on the interstate and had to change it."

That explained the dirt smudges she saw on his dress shirt. "I thought you forgot about our interview," Serenity said, not willing to let him off the hook too easily.

Phillip stretched out his hand, and she took it. As they shook, Phillip said, "I could never forget an appointment with Serenity Williams. Even four flat tires couldn't keep me away."

Serenity pulled her hand out of his grip. The man was charming, but he was a preacher, and that made her mistrustful. It also made him off-limits. Ever since that swollen-headed reverend, Michael Randolph, had dumped her because her ministry was more successful than his, she had sworn off preachers. Even her brother, Larry the egomaniac, freely admitted that he wouldn't be able to handle a wife who made more money or was better known than he. Falling in love with a preacher was for women who looked good in straitjackets and liked padded rooms. Best just to get this interview over with and forget she'd ever met Pastor Phillip McKnight. "So, would you like to talk in here first, or would you like to show the camera crew around the church so they can shoot some footage for the show?"

"Umm…well, I—I guess we could talk first, if—if that's okay with you," Phillip said.

"Are you sure, Pastor McKnight? Because, if you'd rather work with the film crew first, I'm okay with that."

"No, no—please, sit back down. I'd like nothing more than to speak with you right now." He sat down behind his desk and then said, "I forgot to charge my cell phone."

What does that have to do with anything? Serenity wondered as she looked at him with questioning eyes.

Phillip pulled his cell phone out of his pocket and set it on his desk. "I would have called to tell you that I was going to be late, but my cell died on me."

"Okay," Serenity said. She had already moved on and wished he'd do the same. She pulled her notepad and pen out of her purse. "This is a pretty big church building for such a young ministry. Most preachers begin their ministries in storefronts or other smaller locales. What made you decide to go so big so soon?"

"No small talk, no chitchat; just get straight down to business, huh?"

Serenity put down her notepad. "I wasn't trying to rush you, Pastor McKnight. It's just that my father taught me about the value of time, and I try not to waste it."

"Your father seems like a wise man. That's why I have a meeting scheduled with him next week. I'll be sure to let him know that his daughter still follows his advice."

Serenity's curiosity was piqued. She wanted to know why Pastor Phillip McKnight would leave the warmth of Tampa, Florida, to come to Chicago during the season of snowstorms and winter chills, but she didn't ask. Instead, she said, "Make sure to bring a heavy coat and a pair of gloves. They don't call it the Windy City for nothing."

"I plan to. Your father already warned me about the weather. But he promised that your mother would fix a warm meal for my trouble."

With a furrowed brow, Serenity said, "My mother normally tells me when she and my father are hosting out-of-town guests. I'm surprised she didn't say anything about your visit." Then, as if shaking off the shocking news, she picked her notepad back up. "Shall we continue, then, Pastor McKnight?"

Phillip put his elbows on his desk and smiled at her. "Would you do me a favor?" he asked.

"That depends. What do you need?" she asked with a wary grin on her face.

"Would you please call me Phillip? I don't think we need to be so formal, especially since I'll be meeting your parents next week."

Okay, the suspense was killing her. There was no way she was going to be able to wait until she was finished with her work to call her mother and find out why Phillip was coming to dinner. "So, why are you and my father getting together next week?"

"I guess I'm kind of looking for a spiritual father, of sorts. I've been a pastor for only two years, and I'm getting to the point where I really need some godly guidance and mentoring."

"Are you saying that you've decided to voluntarily bring the church you built under another man's leadership?"

Phillip shook his head. "I don't see it as the church I built. This church was built by God and the people of God, and I just want to continue to honor Him in all that we do."

Most of the pastors Serenity knew weren't eager to submit themselves to another man's leadership. Michael, for example, had always complained about the things her father would ask him to do when he'd presided over Michael's church. Even her thickheaded brother complained about their dad poking his nose into his business from time to time. Serenity had to admit, Pastor Phillip McKnight seemed somewhat different. But there had to be something wrong with him—after all, his ex-wife had left him for some reason, right?

Serenity had finally agreed to do this interview in part because she'd figured it would give her an opportunity to show her viewers how egotistical and pride-filled Pastor McKnight was. This might just be her chance. She leaned closer to Phillip and, in the most innocent voice she could muster, said, "You sound like a reasonable man, Pastor McKnight. One would wonder why your wife divorced you."

Phillip flinched, then said, "I've got an idea. Why don't you wait for me in the sanctuary? I'll change my shirt, and then we can give the camera crew a tour of the facility while you interview me about the ministry."

She didn't miss his emphasis on "about the ministry," and she was immediately horrified at what she'd said.

Phillip had changed the subject, and she was more than willing to move away from it, as well. "You keep extra shirts at work?" she asked.

Phillip stood up and pointed at the dirt spots on his shirt. "Never know when I'll get all grimy changing a tire."

"My father keeps extra clothes at his church office, too."

"Smart man," Phillip said.

She laughed as she stood up. "Okay, I'll wait for you in the sanctuary."

Before she could turn away, Phillip said, "You have a beautiful smile, Serenity. You should always keep a smile on your face."

The compliment made Serenity uncomfortable. She turned and headed out the door as quick as her three-inch heels would carry her.

⌒

Why did I say that? Phillip wanted to bash himself in the head for speaking like that to a woman who obviously wanted nothing to do with him. Serenity Williams had practically run out of his office, as if he'd told her he had swine flu or something.

Phillip took off his soiled shirt, reached into his closet, and grabbed a blue button-down. As he put it on and then turned to the mirror to examine himself, his thoughts turned back to Serenity. He had been watching her program for more than a month now—not every day, but he made a point to watch whenever he could. Somehow, he'd never imagined that her hazel eyes would sparkle as brightly as they did in person. And that smile of hers almost took his breath away. Actually, Phillip wished it had taken his breath away, for then, he wouldn't have been able to embarrass himself with stupid talk.

How could he have come on to Serenity like some high school jock with a crush on the prom queen? He lightly slapped his cheeks with his fingertips. "Get yourself together. Go out there and act in a professional manner," he instructed himself, pointing a finger at his reflection in the mirror.

Phillip left his office, determined to conduct himself in an upright way. Serenity might very well be one of the most beautiful women he'd seen in a long time, but he was a man of God, and he knew how to control himself. "Okay," Phillip said, clasping his hands together as he stood in the sanctuary, looking from Serenity to the camera crew. "Is everybody ready to get this tour started?"

"We sure are." Serenity stood up and introduced Phillip to the camera crew, which consisted of two guys. "This is Lenny," she said as she pointed to a tall, slim Conan O'Brien look-alike. "He'll be snapping pictures." She then pointed to a slightly balding African-American man wearing blue jeans and a shirt with palm trees on it. "Bob will be shooting all the footage."

"Hello, Lenny. Hello, Bob." Phillip nodded at each man.

"So, where do you want to start?" Serenity asked him.

"Well, you're already in my pride and joy." Phillip lifted his arms and did a full circle on the plush carpet of the sanctuary. "This is the first space that was finished, after the office complex. We wanted to be able to have services here, even while the construction crew was pounding their way through the rest of the building."

Serenity looked from the pulpit to the many pews that lined the first floor and then to the balcony. "This is a beautiful sanctuary. I love the navy and burgundy colors you chose. Very bold, but still warm and inviting." She turned to Phillip and asked, "How many people can you fit in this sanctuary?"

"It seats about three thousand."

"For such a young ministry, that is an awful lot of members to have."

"Oh, we have only about eighteen hundred members, but I believe that we will quickly grow into the place."

"Sources have said that you put up five million of your own money for this project, but I'm surprised that a bank would loan you the rest of the money you needed without the membership to back it up," Serenity said.

"I'm still raising capital to finish the building. We're a work in progress, as you will see."

"So, the bank wouldn't loan you the money?"

"We're in a recession. They loaned me half of what I needed, and I have to come up with the other half."

"But you've already put up so much of your own money. Do you think you'll get to a point where you'll say enough is enough?"

Shaking his head, Phillip said, "I would give that and much more to the vision God gave me." What he didn't say, though, was that following God's purpose for his life had already cost him dearly. He had been willing to give the money, but watching his wife walk out the door had been the hardest thing he'd ever done. "Let's move forward, shall we?"

Phillip led them to the office suite and let them snap pictures of the staff members as they went about their various tasks. Then, he showed them the spaces that would one day be the youth center, additional classrooms, and the fitness room.

"I have never seen a fitness room in a church complex," Serenity said, signaling Lenny to continue snapping pictures of the equipment.

Phillip picked a fifty-pound weight off the floor and put it back on the rack where it belonged. Although the room was not yet finished, several men in the church had set up the equipment and begun using it, anyway. Guys didn't need much—just some barbells and a bench press. Ladies, on the other hand, would want to pretty the room up, get rid of the dust and clutter, hang mirrors, and so forth. "I believe in the importance of staying in shape—taking care of God's temple," he said.

"I guess you do," Serenity said with a thoughtful look on her face. Then, she snapped back into professional mode with another question. "So, what does a day in the life of Phillip McKnight look like?"

"I'm not very complex. I get up around six in the morning. I go for a run, then I dig into the Word of God and pray, have a quick breakfast, and come to the church. Once I'm at church, I either plan my sermon or do some other work around here."

"Speaking of your sermon," Serenity said, "what time do you want us back here tonight so that Bob can film the message?"

"The service begins at seven, but I normally don't start preaching until about seven forty-five."

"Okay," Serenity said as she held out her hand to shake Phillip's. "I think we got some good footage today.

So, we'll wrap up for now and finish everything this evening."

As Phillip took Serenity's hand in his, he had to remind himself that this was a business meeting and not a first date. He wanted to kiss her hand, but he restrained himself. When he released her hand, he noticed the Gucci watch on her wrist. His ex-wife had liked expensive things, too, and he couldn't help wondering if Serenity was just like the woman who'd left him and taken half of his hard-earned money with her.

Two

"WHY DIDN'T YOU TELL ME THAT YOU'RE HAVING a dinner party on Friday?" Serenity asked her mother, First Lady Evelyn Williams, over the phone during her lunch break.

"I'm lucky your father told me! I didn't find out until you had already left for Tampa," Evelyn told her daughter.

"Phillip wants Daddy to be the presiding bishop of his church, so you'd better fix one of your famous pasta dishes."

"Oh, I don't have to go to all that trouble—I can serve peanut butter and jelly sandwiches if my beautiful daughter shows up. That man will lose his mind and do whatever Lawrence tells him."

Serenity rolled her eyes. "Mom, I have told you a hundred times, I am through with ego-driven preachers."

"Well, I married a preacher, and things turned out all right for me," her mother said in a pouty tone.

"Daddy is the exception to the rule. But that bigheaded brother of mine is another matter altogether."

Her mother laughed. "You better stop talking about my son, girl. You know I don't play that. And what about Melinda's husband? He seems like a really good catch."

Yes, he was a good catch. But Melinda, her best friend, had waited ten years for Steven Marks to come to his senses. Serenity simply didn't have that kind of patience.

"Whatever," Serenity said with a sigh. She turned and saw her producer, Pam Norman, heading in her direction. "Look, Mom, I've got to get going. I was working on some edits with Pam, and she just got back from lunch."

"Okay, so I'll see you Friday, right?"

"I'll be at the house for the Super Bowl on Sunday, for sure, but I'm not making any promises about Friday." She saw Pam disappear into the editing room. "I'll talk to you later, Mom." She hung up and then went to join Pam. Her producer had been the one to suggest doing the interview with Phillip McKnight. According to her, Christian women dreamed about marrying gorgeous preachers, and she figured that unprecedented numbers of viewers would tune in to see Phillip McKnight's handsome face—and, of course, to hear everything he had to say.

"Will you look at that man?" Pam said, practically drooling over the image of Phillip on the monitor. "I know he's a preacher, but Lord, help me, Jesus."

They were watching the footage of Phillip preaching. His sermon had been electrifying that night. He had spoken about loving Jesus with one's heart like a drug addict searching out his next fix—with hunger. Serenity had to admit, she liked his style. She didn't know exactly how much he had earned throughout his football career, but it had to have been a lot, especially if the man had been willing to put five million dollars from his own pocket toward building that church. His sacrifice impressed her, made her want to know more about him. But she would never admit that to anyone.

"What do you think?" Pam asked as she turned away from the screen to look at Serenity.

"He's all right."

"Oh, please—that man is so much more than just 'all right.' I can feel the Holy Spirit moving, even through the screen, so I know you felt it while you were sitting in that sanctuary."

"I guess I'm just jaded. I've heard pastors preach like Bishop Jakes and dance like King David, only to come down from the pulpit and treat other people like dirt."

"Did Pastor McKnight seem like that kind of person?"

Serenity leaned back in her seat and thought about her encounter with Phillip McKnight. He hadn't acted as if the world and all the people in it had been put there just to serve him. In fact, he seemed quite the opposite. In a word: humble. "No, he didn't seem like that kind of person at all."

☙

"What am I doing?" Serenity asked herself on Friday evening as she prepared to go to her parents' dinner party. She looked at her reflection in the mirror and admired her knee-length, Italian silk dress by Versace. It was a two-thousand-dollar dress that she had found in a secondhand shop for a little less than two hundred bucks—a deal that she just hadn't been able to pass up. She loved designer clothes yet would never dream of paying full price for items that were here today but could be gone tomorrow. Rather than splurge on trendy attire, she preferred bargain hunting so she could use more of her money for kingdom building.

She put on her wrap and walked out the door with more anticipation than she'd felt about anything in a long time. *Get yourself together, girl. You're not going on a date with Phillip. Your parents and brothers will be there, too*, Serenity reminded herself as she drove down the street, heading to her parents' house.

She still didn't understand why she was so excited about seeing Phillip again. He was all wrong for her. Michael had shown her how foolish she had been to put her faith and trust in an ego-driven preacher, who hadn't been able to handle her success or the fact that more people recognized her than him. Why couldn't he have just accepted the fact that her success was from God's hands? It was clearly God's will that her ministry succeed, so how could Michael have just rejected her like that?

"Lord, please help me," Serenity prayed as she parked her car in front of the Williams' house. "I feel like I'm becoming so bitter because of how Michael treated me. I don't want to be bitter. I need You to help me get over this." When she finished praying, she got out of the car, marched up the walkway, and entered through the front door, resolving to leave yesterday outside.

ஒ

Phillip had determined not to look into Serenity's eyes tonight. Her eyes had mesmerized him the last time he'd seen her and caused him to say stupid things. It was obvious that she wanted nothing to do with him, but he hadn't been able to stop himself from throwing one compliment after another at her until he had made her so uncomfortable that she'd rushed out of his office.

Phillip had reclaimed his senses now. Serenity might be beautiful, but it seemed to him that she was just like his ex-wife, Chantel. As far as he was concerned, there was nothing wrong with wanting the best out of life. But Chantel had wanted a big, beautiful house, a Mercedes, *and* a Jaguar. She'd demanded fur coats and designer clothes; and Phillip had freely given her everything her heart desired. However, Chantel had not been so generous with him. When Phillip had decided to put his own money toward building God's house, she had run to a divorce lawyer and demanded half of all his earnings. In the end, she'd taken ten million of his hard-earned savings and walked out of his life as if he'd never meant a thing to her.

When Phillip had seen that high-priced Gucci watch on Serenity's wrist, and when she'd commented about the five million he'd spent to build the church, he'd imagined that she and Chantel were probably cut from the same cloth. So, it was better to just keep things moving and stay away from Serenity's mesmerizing eyes.

"So, what did you think about what my father had to say today?" asked Larry Williams, the firstborn son of Lawrence and Evelyn Williams and heir to the Williams pastoral dynasty.

"I appreciated everything he said. I know that my divorce puts a stain on my reputation, but it wasn't something I initiated. I wasn't chasing skirts behind Chantel's back or slapping her around. As a matter of fact, she was the one who was unfaithful to me. But I guess her boyfriend didn't have enough money, because she still wanted to get her piece of the pie before I spent it all building something for God."

"Man, that stinks."

"Tell me about it. I thought Chantel was marrying me because of love, but it turned out she loved my money and couldn't bear to see it spent on anyone—or anything—but her."

"That's exactly why I'm still single. Dad is always harping on me to get married, but, with my taste in women, I'd probably marry someone like your ex-wife. I'm not sure I could deal with that."

"Hey, Dad said y'all need to break up this huddle and come socialize with the rest of us," Monroe said as he approached Phillip and Larry.

Larry turned to Phillip. "Are you sure you want to be a part of this ministry? My father can be very demanding," he said with a wink.

"Yeah," affirmed Monroe, "he once made a pastor stand before his congregation and apologize for neglecting his wife for the ministry." Monroe turned and looked at his wife, Cathy, who was sitting by herself at the dining room table. He then turned back to the men and said, "Let's just say, I'm glad I'm not a preacher."

"But you are a politician, little brother. So, be careful, or the old man might have you stand before your constituents and rededicate yourself to Cathy."

Before Monroe could respond, the front door opened, and Phillip was once again caught in a whirlwind as he watched Serenity walk into the house, take off her wrap, and hang it in the closet. The dress she wore was simple in its cut and design, but Phillip had bought enough designer dresses for Chantel to know real quality when he saw it. Serenity had expensive taste. That fact alone calmed the whirlwind and helped Phillip to begin thinking sensibly again. He couldn't afford another ten-million-dollar divorce settlement, and he would do well to remember that.

The three men walked over to join Bishop Williams and Lady Evelyn, who stood talking with Daniel Matthew, the pastor of a church within Bishop Williams's fellowship. Bishop Williams turned to Phillip. "My sons aren't filling your head with horror stories, are they?"

"No sir, it all sounds good to me," Phillip responded. A little heavy-handedness was all right with him. His father had died a year after he was born, so he had missed the firm discipline of a man during those impressionable years. Luckily for him, his mother was no pushover; that fact, along with his being enrolled in a football program from an early age, had aided in guiding him in the right direction. But, now that Phillip was a pastor, he wanted his church to be presided over by a man who stood unswervingly on the principles of God. From what he could see, Bishop Lawrence Williams was such a man.

Serenity greeted everyone as she approached, then turned to Phillip. "So, I see you've had a chance to meet Larry and Moe. Too bad Curly won't be here tonight."

"Who?" Phillip asked with raised eyebrows.

"That's Serenity's name for Jay," Larry chimed in. "She calls us Larry, Moe, and Curly, like The Three Stooges." He rolled his eyes. "You'll have to excuse my sister. She is the corniest talk show host I know."

"We've gone through this before, Larry. I'm not a talk show host. My program is about ministry. I preach, but I also interview other ministers."

"Whatever you want to call it, little sis. I just think your ministry gift is being wasted on television. You should be the pastor of your own church."

"I have more than a million viewers, Larry. How many members attend your church, huh?" She didn't wait for an answer but swirled on her heels and walked into the dining room, where she began talking to Cathy.

"What was that about?" Phillip asked Larry. He'd never seen Serenity's temper before.

"Ah, she gets mad every time I tell her that she needs her own church. My sister is anointed—God knows that. I just don't think she's settled yet."

"Her program is very good. And as she said, she's reaching a lot of people." Phillip didn't know why he felt compelled to speak up for Serenity, but he couldn't let Larry put down her ministry like that.

"Yeah, but she keeps herself away from real commitment by staying behind that television screen. Who does she really connect with?"

Phillip looked in the direction of the dining room and saw Serenity, standing on one side of the table, talking with Cathy, who stayed seated on the other side of the table. He found himself wondering if Larry was right. Did Serenity have a hard time connecting with people? Was she really hiding behind the TV cameras? And, if so, why?

"Okay, Larry. Stop analyzing my daughter," Lady Evelyn said with a stern expression on her face.

Larry lifted his hands in surrender. "I won't say another word about it tonight."

Moments later, they sat down to dinner. Bishop Williams sat at the head of the table, with Lady Evelyn on his right and Larry on his left. Monroe sat next to Larry, with his wife next to him. Phillip had been seated next to Lady Evelyn, and Serenity sat next to him, with Pastor Matthew on her other side.

Bishop Williams prayed over the food, and then everyone started filling their plates. As an only child, Phillip had grown up eating most of his meals on a tray in front of the television while his mother was at work. Consequently, he'd never felt totally comfortable with the table etiquette for dinner parties.

His nervousness must have shown, because Serenity leaned over to him and said, "Just pick up your fork and eat. My mom is a wonderful cook. You have nothing to fear."

"I'm sure it's delicious," Phillip said as he picked up his fork and knife. "And, regarding Curly—I mean, Jay—I already know your youngest brother. I'll be seeing him in

Miami on Sunday." Jay Williams played for the New Orleans Saints. He and Phillip had met during Phillip's final
years as the Bucs' quarterback. Their teams had played
against each other once, and Phillip's team had won.

"You're going to the Super Bowl?" Serenity exclaimed.
She turned to Lady Evelyn. "Mom, Phillip's going to the
Super Bowl!"

"I know, dear. He told us earlier."

Sounding awestruck, Serenity said, "Man, I wish I had
planned to go. I would have, if I'd thought that the Saints
would actually be playing."

Breaking with his habitual seriousness, Bishop Williams started the Saints' rally cry. "Who dat, who dat?"

"The Colts are favored to win this game, so don't get
your hopes up too high, Dad," Monroe said.

"Win or lose, this is amazing," Serenity put in. "I
mean, come on! The Saints—formerly known as the
Ain'ts—have never been to the Super Bowl. I'm proud of
Jay for sticking it out through the tough years."

"You like football?" Phillip asked. He was just a little
surprised.

"Are you kidding? Around here, it's always been Jesus
and football. I probably would have gotten scalped if I'd
tried to change the channel when I was a teenager. So, I
learned to put on my sweats and holler with the rest of
them."

"I guess you all get pretty wild during football season,
then?" Phillip asked.

"Jay is the wild one of this bunch," Serenity said.

Phillip had seen the headlines about Jay, but he saw
more in the young man than what had been widely reported. "He'll come around. Jay loves your father, and he
loves the Lord. So, I wouldn't worry about him."

Bishop Williams stood up and made a toast, and then the conversation began flowing around the table. Phillip was having a good time, and he hadn't allowed himself to gaze into Serenity's eyes once the entire evening.

"Since you and Dad don't meet until two o'clock tomorrow, I can pick you up at your hotel and take you to breakfast," Larry said to Phillip.

Phillip liked that idea very much. He could already tell that he and Larry were going to get along just fine. "Sounds good to me."

Serenity sat up a bit straighter and added, "If you have time after breakfast, Larry can drop you at the television station so that we can go over the edits on your show. We'll be airing it next week."

Phillip turned to Larry. "Do you think you can get me to Serenity's studio after breakfast?"

"Not a problem," Larry assured him.

"I'll drop Phillip at the church before your meeting, okay, Dad?" Serenity offered.

"Thanks, baby girl. And thank you, too, Larry. It looks like Phillip is in good hands with the Williams family." The Bishop leaned back in his seat, looking full and happy.

Three

EVERY MORNING, BEFORE THE DAY BECAME TOO HEC-
tic, Serenity picked up her Bible and studied the
Word of God. This morning, she had combed
through several psalms and several passages in Proverbs,
and now she was reading from the book of John. She was
struck by verses 31 and 32 of chapter eight: *"Then Jesus
said to those Jews who believed Him, 'If you abide in My
word, you are My disciples indeed. And you shall know
the truth, and the truth shall make you free.'"*

For reasons she couldn't identify or explain, she felt
that the Lord had guided her to that particular passage.
There was something that God was trying to show her.
But she would have to figure that out later, because she
was running late. Larry had told her that he would drop
Phillip at the studio by ten, and she didn't want to keep
them waiting, since Phillip had a meeting with her father
that very afternoon.

She showered and threw on a purple and white Nike
jogging suit and a pair of white Nike tennis shoes, then
pulled back her hair and tied it up with a hair band. They
never filmed shows on Saturdays, so, when she went into
the studio on the weekend, she liked to dress casually and
comfortably. She made it to the studio by nine thirty, set
up the equipment in the viewing room, and then loaded
the disc of Phillip's show into the DVD player. When the

doorbell rang at five minutes before ten, Serenity went to answer it.

As she opened the door, Larry said, "Tag, you're it," and handed Phillip off to her.

"Don't worry; I'll have him to the church on time."

"You'd better. He and Dad have a lot to go over," Larry said, then gave Phillip a parting pat on the back.

"I guess I've been warned," Serenity said as a burst of cold air blew into the studio. She closed the door and walked Phillip toward the viewing room.

"Thanks for telling me to dress warm," Phillip remarked.

"You can put your hat and coat in here," she told him, indicating a closet.

Phillip took off his gloves and unbuttoned his coat, then hung them inside the closet before following her into the viewing room. "You've gotten everything set up?"

"Yes, sir. I wouldn't want to make you late because you had to wait on me."

"I appreciate that. Someone once told me that Bishop Williams doesn't like to waste other people's time, so I sure don't want to be late and waste his time."

"That would be awful," Serenity said with a smile.

"Especially since I'm trying so hard to impress the man."

She sat down on the couch and invited Phillip to join her. "So, you've made your decision? The honorable Bishop Lawrence Williams will preside over your church?"

Phillip sat down next to her. "I met with two other bishops. They were both great guys, but I really feel that God is telling me this is the fellowship where I belong."

"Well, you picked a fine man to be your bishop. And I'm not just saying that because I'm his daughter, either.

I'm one of his parishioners, and I've found that my father lives an exemplary life." After that vote of confidence
for her father, Serenity turned her attention to work. She
picked up the remote and pressed PLAY. "We start with
you preaching and then cut away to our conversation."

After watching the tape for a few minutes, Phillip
said, "You showed only a couple minutes of the sermon.
Will the rest of the show cover the interview?"

"This is going to be a three-day series," Serenity explained. She didn't tell him that her producer had suggested spreading the interview over three days with the
reasoning that more women would tune in to watch the
show once they'd witnessed the anointing in his sermon
and seen how fine he was. "We're going to show bits and
pieces of the interview and your sermon on the first day.
The second day, we'll show the tour of your facilities, and,
on the third, we'll show the rest of your sermon."

"It sounds like you've got it mapped out pretty good.
I'm just surprised that you're giving me so much airtime."

"My producer felt that we would gain more viewers
by spreading the feature over three days." Serenity turned
away from Phillip, hoping he wouldn't catch the under-
lying reason—that they thought more and more women
would watch.

"That's great. I just didn't think I would receive so
much coverage."

"I figured that we could sell some of your ministry
tapes at the end of each broadcast as a way of raising
funds for your building project." Serenity thought that
was the least she could do, since Pam was shamelessly
using Phillip to boost their ratings.

"I appreciate that," Phillip said. "I've been trying to
figure out a way to finish the building without depleting
my children's inheritance."

Serenity had been watching the edited version of the program as she talked to Phillip, but the minute she heard him mention his children, she swiveled around to face him. "I didn't know you had children."

He raised an eyebrow. "I didn't know you cared."

Serenity turned back to the television, trying to project nonchalance. "I don't, really. It was just a question."

"Well, to answer your question, I don't have any children. But I want to have them. Hopefully, it will happen for me one day."

Serenity kept her eyes on the viewing screen and her mouth shut. She had already pried into Phillip's business more than a professional acquaintance should. So, she was not about to open her mouth, lest she inadvertently ask something else inappropriate. When they finished viewing the edited tapes, she stood up. "So, what do you think?"

"I like it! You and your producer did an excellent job with the edits. I'll get together the ministry series that I'd like to promote on the show and send that information to you early next week."

◆

"Well, if there's nothing else—" Serenity's cell phone rang, cutting her off. She checked the caller ID, then smiled and opened the phone. "This is Serenity," she said, then paused to listen. Phillip could hear chatter on the other end but couldn't make out specific words.

"You're kidding, right?...Well, hold on to it; I'll be right there." She hung up the phone, looked at her watch, and then turned back to Phillip. "I promise I won't make you late, but I need you to ride with me somewhere, okay?"

"As long as we can make it to the church by two, I'm all yours," Phillip said.

"Okay. Grab your coat, and let's hit the road. It's twelve thirty right now, and even though the Chicago traffic is horrendous, I'm sure I'll get you to New Hope on time."

"Where are we going?" Phillip asked once they were driving down the street.

"To High Gloss. They're having a sample sale, and one of the clerks spotted a Jully Kang dress that's just my size." She jubilantly pumped her fist in the air.

"I've never heard of Jully Kang."

"That's why High Gloss is unique. They deal with independent designers and Chicago locals, so shoppers get designer clothes at discounted prices. It's like buying the Versace of tomorrow at Wal-Mart prices." The excitement was still in her voice as she went on to talk about her favorite discount designers.

"You really love to shop, don't you?"

"Are you kidding?" Serenity smiled sheepishly. "I'll admit, I'm a little addicted. It's a passion that my mother cultivated in me when I was a kid. But, in her defense, we never spent more than fifty bucks on our Saturday morning shopping sprees."

Phillip laughed incredulously. "How can it be a true shopping spree if you spend only fifty bucks? That won't buy you more than a belt!"

"When I was growing up, my dad was just starting out in the ministry, and he and my mom didn't have much money," Serenity explained. "So, Mom dealt with her shopping addiction by seeking out every thrift store in the Chicago area. She and I would go from store to store trying to find fabulous bargains for our family."

"So, Jay wore hand-me-downs, huh? Just wait till I see him on Sunday," Phillip joked.

"Hey, don't knock hand-me-downs. Some of my best deals were pre-owned."

"Like what?" Phillip asked, wanting to keep up their lighthearted banter.

"Okay, Mr. Smarty-Pants, I'll tell you. Do you remember the dress I wore to dinner last night?"

"Yes. And I could tell it was expensive, so I know you couldn't have gotten too great a deal on it."

"It was Versace. Normally two thousand dollars. But I bought it at a secondhand shop for less than two hundred bucks." Serenity smiled smugly. "I love designer clothes, but I love discounts even more. It's one trait of my mom's that I'm proud to have inherited."

Phillip pointed at her wrist. "I thought you were going to tell me you got a good deal on this Gucci watch."

Turning off the highway, Serenity glanced down at the timepiece and grinned. "I did haggle the man a lot over the price, but I didn't get as good a deal on this watch as I would have liked. Still, I had extenuating circumstances for buying it. And even my mother, the queen of hagglers, agreed with me."

"What extenuating circumstances could you possibly have for buying a Gucci watch?" Phillip asked, incredulous.

"I was on my honeymoon—by myself."

"Ouch," Phillip said, nodding empathetically. He hoped she wasn't offended.

Just then, Serenity pulled the car into a parking space. "I'll be right back," she said before jumping out of the car.

Two minutes later, she returned, carrying a dress bag. "Let me see what you raced down here to get," Phillip said when she got into the car.

Serenity opened the bag and displayed a long, midnight-black evening gown. "Satisfied?"

"Not yet. How much did you pay for it?"

"Guess."

"Hmm…one hundred?"

"Nope." She giggled. "Just sixty-four bucks."

"Didn't you tell me that your mom never spent more than fifty bucks on a shopping spree? Yet, you bought only one dress with a price tag that exceeds your mother's limit. I'm going to have to tell Lady Evelyn about this," Phillip joked.

"My mother doesn't wear designer clothes. She is of the mind-set that, if it fits, then it's just fine. That's okay for her, because she looks wonderful in everything she puts on. But her daughter just happens to like designer clothes—at bargain prices, of course."

"Okay," he said, holding up his hands in surrender. "I won't tell."

"My mother wouldn't say anything, anyway. Now, my best friend, Melinda? She's the one who thinks I need therapy. Melinda would rather walk into Saks, buy the first outfit she likes, and leave within fifteen minutes rather than spend hours scouring the racks for a bargain." Serenity looked at her watch again. "It's ten after one. I've got fifty minutes to get you on the other side of town. But, don't worry—we'll make it."

Phillip leaned back in his seat. "I trust you," he said.

In a strange way, finding out about Serenity's propensity to save money made Phillip trust her more, and he was enjoying spending time with her more than he'd expected to. She seemed so much more relaxed in her studio than she had been at his church or even at her parents' house the night before. "So, what else do you do for fun, Serenity?" he asked, wanting to know more about her.

"I don't have time for any other addictions. I really want *Walk This Way* to be a success, so I'm constantly working on the show."

"What does success look like to you?"

Serenity honked her horn as a driver cut in front of her. "Well, it's not the viewership that determines success to me, although I wouldn't be mad if I had Oprah's ratings. But I'm more interested in helping people understand the Bible and the ways that God desires for us to handle our unique Christian walks."

"So, that's why you named the program *Walk This Way*—because you're helping people figure out how to walk with God?"

"Exactly!" Serenity shook her head. "None of my brothers got it. They kept telling me that *Walk This Way* sounded stupid, and that no one would get it. I had to remind them that it couldn't be that stupid—Ed Young's radio broadcast is called *Winning Walk*."

"Your family seems pretty close-knit," Phillip remarked.

"We are. But, every now and then, I have to put Larry, Moe, and Curly in their place. Being the only girl, I learned early on how to get out of headlocks and how to keep meddling brothers from getting too deep into my business."

"You sure put Larry in his place last night. 'I have over a million viewers; how many church members do you have?'" Phillip mimicked her in a high-pitched voice.

Serenity laughed. "Oh, he deserved it. He's always getting on my case about the route of ministry I've chosen, but I don't see him getting on Monroe for going into politics or Jay about going into professional sports rather than becoming pastors."

"Yeah, but that's different. You're a minister, and your other two brothers aren't."

He watched as Serenity gripped the wheel as she jerked a hard right to get into the slow lane and exit the highway. "Don't tell me that you're on Larry's side. What did he tell you at breakfast this morning?"

"Slow down, Serenity. Your brother didn't tell me anything. And I'm not on anyone's side in this matter. I was just making a conjecture as to why Larry doesn't hound Monroe and Jay about getting involved in the ministry."

Serenity seemed to calm back down. "Sorry if I jerked you around. I didn't mean to swing the car into the other lane so fast."

"You might need some counseling for that temper of yours, but I'm okay. I won't be suing you for whiplash this time."

"Well, you won't have another chance to call your attorney, because we have arrived at our destination. We'll pull into the parking lot of New Hope as soon as I make this turn."

Phillip watched as the mammoth-sized church came into view. The outside was covered in white stone, with a gold cross hanging directly above the front doors of the church.

Serenity pulled into a parking space and put the car in park, then looked down at her watch and smiled. "One minute to spare. Didn't I tell you I'd get you here on time?"

Never in Phillip's life had he ever desired to be late for an appointment that mattered to him. But he realized he would have given anything for another minute with Serenity.

Four

A S SERENITY WAS PULLING OUT OF THE CHURCH PARK-
ing lot after dropping Phillip off, she received
a call from her mother. "Did you get Phillip to
your dad on time?" her mother asked her.

"Yes, Mom. I'm just leaving the church now."

"Oh, good. Why don't you come over to the house and
help me with something?"

Serenity didn't have anything else planned for the
day, and she'd thought she might clean her house. But
she was more than willing to put that off for another day.
"What did you have in mind?"

"I promised Sister Allen and Sister Stokes that I would
bring some banana nut bread to church tomorrow. I
thought you might like to help me in the kitchen today."

"As long as I get to take a loaf home with me, I'm in."

"Of course you can, honey. We'll make one for Phillip
to take home, too."

"I'm on my way," Serenity said. She closed her cell
phone and then drove to her parents' house, which was
only five minutes from New Hope Church.

While she and her mother were making a mess in the
kitchen, the phone rang, and her mother answered it. "Hi,
honey….Let me check with Serenity."

Her mother put her hand over the mouthpiece of the
phone. "Would you like to help your father and me give
Phillip a tour of our city this afternoon?"

46

Serenity stopped stirring the batter and shook her head no.

Her mother took her hand off the phone. "We'd love to go. The bread should be done in an hour, so pick us up anytime after that."

When her mother hung up the phone, Serenity asked, "Why did you tell them that I would go?"

"You need to get out more. You're so busy with your television ministry and speaking engagements that I'm worried you're forgetting to take time for yourself. So, today, you're just going to relax and hang out with your parents and Phillip. Okay?"

"Okay, Mom, but only because I didn't have anything better to do, anyway."

⸎

"What time does your flight leave?" Serenity asked Phillip. He was sitting next to her in the backseat of the Williams' SUV, and the Bishop was driving Lady Evelyn and them toward downtown Chicago.

"I'm taking the red-eye out tonight. I have a guest speaker coming to my church tomorrow, but I'm still going home for the service. After that, I'll head to Miami for the game."

"Tell Jay I'm rooting for him," Serenity said.

"I'll do that."

"So, where are we headed first, Daddy?" Serenity asked, leaning forward to be heard up front.

"Phillip tells me that he doesn't know much about our great city, so I'm going to drive by a few places and start with a little history lesson."

Serenity turned back to Phillip and chuckled. "You're in for it now. My father is a history buff. You never should have told him that you don't know much about Chicago."

"Ignore Serenity," Lady Evelyn said, turning around in her seat. "You'll enjoy this tour. We'll even take you to Little Italy so you can enjoy some Chicago-style pizza."

"That's right!" Serenity said. "You haven't had pizza until you've had Chicago's deep dish."

"I'm actually not much of a pizza eater," Phillip admitted. "I had so much of it when I played football that it's taking me a while to develop a taste for it again."

"Understood," Bishop Williams said. "Well, how about a Chicago dog, then?"

"That sounds great," Phillip said. Breakfast had been a while ago, and he was beginning to get hungry.

Minutes later, Bishop Williams pulled into the parking lot of a strip mall. "This place has great hotdogs. Let's eat, and then we can officially begin the tour."

After a quick lunch, they got back in the SUV and headed to their first stop, the Willis Tower. "Now this, young man, is the tallest building in the United States and the fifth tallest in the world. It used to be called the Sears Tower, and it stands a hundred and ten stories high."

"Wow," Phillip said, leaning back so he could see the top of the tower. "The tallest building we have in Tampa is only forty-two stories high."

"Well, Chicago has a reputation to uphold—the first skyscraper in the world was built here in 1885. It was only ten stories high, but, since then, cities and countries all over the world have been competing with us. We've got a new building going up that will be two thousand and eleven feet tall, beating out the building New York intends to replace the Twin Towers with by about eleven feet," Bishop Williams said.

After they'd seen the Willis Tower, Bishop Williams drove to the Trump Tower and then to the John Hancock

Center. In the lobby of the John Hancock Center, they passed a group of people who looked like tourists. Two of the men stopped in their tracks, turned around, and started shouting, "McKnight! McKnight, is that you?"

Phillip turned around and waved, walking to meet the group. "You caught me," he said with a chuckle, shaking hands with the men. "Yes, I'm Phillip McKnight."

"Man, where have you been? Tampa hasn't been the same since you retired," one of the men said.

"You're crazy," Phillip said. "The Bucs are doing just fine. I attend as many games as I can manage. They don't appear to be slipping to me."

Another man said, "I heard you became a preacher. Is that true?"

Phillip nodded. "Sure did. I'm running touchdowns for the Lord now."

"That's all right," the third man said as he gave Phillip a good-natured slap on the back.

As they continued talking, Phillip saw one of the women break away from the group and walk over to Serenity. "Hey, aren't you Serenity Williams?" she asked.

"Yes, I am," Serenity replied.

"I love your show—I watch it all the time!" the woman exclaimed.

"Thank you," Phillip heard Serenity say. "I'm glad you enjoy the show." Out of the corner of his eye, he watched as she turned her back on the woman and directed Lady Evelyn into a gift shop.

"I think my party is ready to go, but it was nice talking to you guys," Phillip said. "Keep watching Tampa, because they are going back to the Super Bowl someday."

"So you say," and "Sure, sure," murmured the men as their group moved along.

As Phillip followed Serenity and her parents out of the John Hancock Center, he leaned over and asked her, "What was that all about?"

"What?" Serenity asked, as if she didn't have the slightest idea what he was talking about.

"You brushed off that woman as if she was bothering you."

Serenity stopped and put her hands on her hips. "I did not. I told her that I appreciated her comment. I didn't know the woman, so I'm sure she didn't expect me to carry on a conversation with her."

"If you say so," Phillip said with a raised brow.

"Hey, stop picking on me," Serenity said with a playful punch to his arm.

Phillip rubbed his arm and turned to Lady Evelyn, who had stopped with her husband to wait for him and Serenity. "Did you see that? Your daughter is violent."

Lady Evelyn shrugged. "I raised her better than that. I have no idea where she gets her manners."

❦

They piled back into the SUV, and Serenity's father drove them to Grant Park. "This is where President Obama gave his 2008 victory speech. More than two hundred and forty thousand people were in the park that night."

Then, he told Phillip, "Chicago has had a lot to overcome. In the 1800s, it was described as the filthiest city in America. So, we designed a massive sewer system to solve the problem. We had tons of fires, race riots, and gangs all trying to destroy the beauty of my hometown. But Chicago is a city that doesn't quit. And even though I don't agree with some of his policies, I was proud to stand in this park and listen to the first African-American president-elect of these United States."

"It was too cold for me. I stayed home," Serenity's mother admitted.

"Yes, Mom and I watched the event on TV at her house, wrapped in blankets on the couch," Serenity said. "We made hot chocolate and everything, and *still* couldn't get warm enough."

Her mother was somehow prompted to switch gears, for she turned to Phillip and asked, "Did Serenity tell you that she baked the banana nut bread I gave you, herself?"

Phillip glanced at Serenity with a look of surprise. "You know how to bake? Can you cook, too?"

"Boy, please. I was taught by the best. But, to be truthful, my brothers are even better cooks than I am."

"My mother never had time to teach me how to cook. Either I was at football practice, or she was at one of her two jobs," Phillip said.

"That's too bad," Serenity's mother said. "I hope your mother doesn't keep that same schedule today."

"No, ma'am. When I signed my first NFL contract, I convinced her to quit one of her jobs. Seven years later, when I was playing for the Buccaneers, I bought a house in Tampa for my grandmother and my mom, and she declared that she would never work another day in her life. She still volunteers at a few charities and plans events at her church, though."

Back in the car again, Serenity's mother suggested they think about where to have dinner. "I trust you like Chinese food?" her father asked Phillip.

"Oh, yes, sir."

"Then, why don't we head to Chinatown?"

"That sounds like a great idea."

When they arrived in Chinatown, the four of them got out of the car and walked around for about half an hour before going into a restaurant they agreed on.

When they were seated and had ordered their meals, Serenity's father got the conversation going again. "So, we were talking earlier about Phillip's trip to Haiti to help with the hurricane relief efforts. Phillip, tell them what you'd like to do for the Haitian people."

Serenity's ears perked up.

"Well, right now, we're trying to finish building our church in Tampa. But when we're finished with that, I'd like to begin an ongoing fund-raiser to collect money to build churches in Haiti and other underprivileged countries."

"I think that's a wonderful idea, Phillip," Serenity's mother said, beaming.

"I just want to build houses of worship in places where the people really need an opportunity to hear God's Word. My hope is that our little investment will help to save souls."

When the food arrived at their table, Serenity's father blessed the meal, and then they passed around a steaming bowl of rice. Although she was hungry and loved Chinese, Serenity was slightly annoyed by the interruption. Phillip's passion for souls was honorable, and it moved her; she wanted to hear more. Phillip was definitely a man after God's heart, and she respected him for his ministerial vision.

"You're awfully quiet, Serenity," her father commented. "What are you thinking about?"

"Oh, nothing. I was just wondering if you had thought about getting New Hope involved in this church-building project that Phillip's church is planning to take on."

"That's an excellent idea, honey. I would love for New Hope to partner with New Destiny and expand our missions work." He turned to his wife. "Do you think the women's ministry might have some ideas about ways to raise money?"

"I could probably convince them to adopt this as our spring project," Serenity's mother said. Turning to Phillip, she asked, "Have you appointed someone at your church to spearhead this project?"

"I guess I hadn't gotten that far, but I'll let you know as soon as I decide," Phillip said, then sat back in his seat and smiled at Serenity's mother. "I'm glad to see that you work with your husband in the ministry, Lady Evelyn. My ex-wife never wanted anything to do with the church."

"I'm sorry to hear that," she said.

Serenity wondered why Phillip's wife had been so apathetic about the ministry, and she figured asking him straight-out would be the easiest way to know. "It sounds like that really disappointed you. Did you ever try to find out why?"

"She never wanted to talk about it," Phillip said.

"But you held it against her, right?"

"Well, I do think that a pastor's wife should be willing to work side by side in the ministry with him, so, yes, I guess I did have a problem with it," Phillip answered.

Serenity's mother put down her fork, looking as if she'd just had a spark of inspiration. "Serenity, I have an idea. Why don't you help me with this project? You and Phillip already know each other. So, you could work with him to gather the information and provide me with your recommendation for our women's ministry."

Caught off guard by her mother's proposal, Serenity stammered, "I—I don't know if I'll have time to do something like that, Mom."

"Well, Phillip just said that he needs to finish his own building project before he can start anything else. So, why don't you check your schedule and see if you can work this out?" her mother asked.

"Phillip doesn't even know who he's going to appoint to work on this project, and there are dozens of women at New Hope who would love to do this with you," Serenity said, trying to wiggle her way out of the plan as gently as possible.

"Yes, but you have such a heart for missions work. I really think you're the right person for this job," her mother said, taking away her wiggle room.

Serenity was getting frustrated. Her mother knew that she didn't like getting involved with projects that forced her to collaborate with groups of people. She preferred to work alone and get the job done with as little drama as possible. But her mother was practically throwing her into the fray. If she refused to check her schedule, it would look like she didn't have a heart for kingdom building. And that wasn't true at all. She liked Phillip's idea; she just didn't want to work with him on it. But she finally acquiesced. Turning to Phillip, she said, "I'll check my schedule and let you know if I can help coordinate the project."

Phillip grinned. "I would love for New Hope to partner with New Destiny on this, so, if you'd have the time, I'd truly appreciate it."

"Not a problem. I always have time for kingdom building."

Five

"WHO DAT, WHO DAT?" MELINDA CHANTED ON THE other end of the phone line.

"Who dat say they gonna beat dem Saints?" Serenity echoed.

"I just couldn't believe it," Melinda confessed. "Steven kept saying that with a name like the Saints, New Orleans could never be ruled out. But I'd been listening to all the naysayers, and so I watched and worried, praying for Jay the whole time."

"Girl, my mother was on the floor praying from kick-off till halftime. I was so excited for Jay and for New Orleans."

"That just goes to show that you never know what prayer can do."

"Amen to that. I can't believe my little brother is now wearing a Super Bowl ring! He deserves it, though. He hung in there with that team, no matter what anyone else said. And now they're going back to New Orleans with a victory!"

"I was going to call you last night, after the awards ceremony, but I was so tired, I fell asleep."

"All that praying wore you out," Serenity said with a chuckle.

"Actually, the praying had nothing to do with it. I called to give you some good news."

"What's going on, Melinda?"

"I don't want to tell you. I want you to guess."

"You know I'm terrible at guessing games." Then, all of a sudden, a thought struck her, and Serenity screamed, "You're pregnant!"

"You guessed it!"

"I can't believe it. How did this happen?"

"Okay, now, I know you're not married yet, but do I really have to explain to you where babies come from?" Melinda teased her.

"No, silly. I know where babies come from. I just thought you wanted to wait a little while longer. You and Steven celebrated your first anniversary not too long ago."

"We decided that we would welcome a baby whenever God saw fit to give us one."

"Congratulations, Melinda. I am so happy for you. How about Brianna—is she excited about the news?" Brianna was Steven's nine-year-old daughter from a previous marriage. His wife had died in a car accident when Brianna was only five.

"Are you kidding? Brianna is on cloud nine. You would think she was the one having the baby. She's already picking out names and making plans for the nursery," Melinda said with a laugh.

"When's the baby due?"

"August. So, I'll be fat and uncomfortable for the entire summer."

"Yeah, but at least you'll have something more than a cheeseburger to blame for your weight gain," Serenity pointed out.

"Enough about me. How is everything going with you?" Melinda asked.

"I just interviewed Phillip McKnight. My producer thinks our ratings will go through the roof."

"Phillip McKnight—that fine football player-turned-preacher?" Melinda asked.

"The one and only. He's trying to raise money to finish his building project, to which he's already given five million dollars of his own money."

"You're kidding! He must really be serious about kingdom building."

"He is, Melinda. I was very impressed with the look and feel of the church, not to mention the service I attended. The man has got it going on, and he doesn't appear to be puffed up about it at all."

"How do you know? You just met the man, right?"

"I admit that I don't know much about him, but he founded the church himself—nobody handed it to him. He also asked my father to preside as bishop over his church. Phillip says he respects my father and wants to be accountable to someone who is connected to God. Watch the show today, and you'll see what I'm talking about."

"Well, it sounds like he has impressed you. And, these days, that's hard for a preacher man to do."

"Whatever, Melinda. I'm not as hard on men as you think I am."

"You're not hard on men in general, but on men who preach? Girl, you haven't had a good word to say about any of them lately."

"Didn't I just say something nice about Pastor McKnight?"

"One minute ago, he was Phillip. Why so formal now?"

"Girl, if you don't stop messing with me, I'm going to hang up this phone," Serenity said.

"Don't get mad at me, Serenity. I'm just making an observation."

"What's there to observe? I was just trying to tell you that the man seems to have his head on straight."

"But, you have to admit, since you and Michael broke up, this is the first preacher man you've spoken of in such a glowing fashion."

"Trust me, Melinda, there's nothing to our relationship beyond business, and the fact that I respect Phillip's ministry goals."

"Okay, I'll leave you alone about Mr. Right—I mean, Mr. McKnight," Melinda said with a giggle. "I simply want to know: are you ready to become a godmother?"

"Are you kidding? I've waited my whole life for someone to call me godmother. I can't wait to spoil your baby rotten and then send him back home to you when he starts to squirm."

They continued their conversation for several more minutes, and when they said good-bye, Serenity got on her treadmill. She tried to do about a mile every other day before she left for work. It was the only exercise she got in all week, but she was grateful to be able to find time to do it. Her schedule was becoming increasingly hectic with each passing day. Because of the mounting success of *Walk This Way*, she received more and more invitations to various speaking engagements. She prayerfully decided which invitations to accept, trying to limit them to two or three a month, and then let her assistant, Sandy, contact the other ministries with her regrets.

When her mile was complete, Serenity jumped off the treadmill and headed upstairs to shower and get ready for work. When she arrived at the studio, she noticed that everyone seemed unusually energized. The charged atmosphere seemed strange to her, especially since they would be filming today's show without an audience.

Normally, if the audience was pumped, that helped to re-charge the staff after long nights spent working on the program and editing the footage. She found Pam in the editing room and asked, "What gives? Why is everyone so perky today?"

"They can feel it, Serenity." Pam seemed pumped, too. "Over the past few days, as we've been promoting the program featuring Phillip McKnight, our viewership has increased each day we even *mentioned* him. So, we just believe that the viewership is going to go through the roof these next three days, when we actually air his segments."

"Well, if it does, it won't be for the reason you think," Serenity told Pam. "It will be because Phillip has a God-given vision and a hunger for the Lord that I haven't seen in anyone for a long time." Serenity didn't know why the prevailing impression of Phillip McKnight as a gorgeous guy who just happened to be a pastor and had nothing else but looks to offer offended her, but it did.

Pam threw up her hands in surrender. "You're right, Serenity. Pastor McKnight is an anointed man. And I be-lieve that fact is going to come through the screen and hit our viewers on a deeper level than his good looks will."

Serenity sighed. "All I'm saying is, no more of this let's-interview-gorgeous-men-to-increase-ratings policy. I want to bring people on this show who will edify believ-ers and encourage them in their walks with God. Phillip does that with no problem, so let's just focus on that and get off his looks, okay?"

"Okay, okay—gosh, Serenity! I hadn't even brought up how handsome Pastor McKnight is since we edited his pro-gram. I could see that the show was going to be powerful even if the man looked like a frog—which he doesn't."

Serenity looked down and pretended to search for something on her clipboard, wondering as she did if she was the one stuck on Phillip's looks, and not Pam, who obviously had moved on. While she got ready for the show, she kept reminding herself that although Phillip McKnight was clearly someone special to God, he was not special to her. He was just a preacher whom they happened to be highlighting on her show for the purpose of raising funds for building the kingdom of God.

After she'd put on her freshly ironed, olive-green business suit and had her makeup applied, Serenity awaited her cue, then stepped onto the set. With the cameras trained on her, she greeted the imaginary audience and said, "Have we got a show for you today! I've been telling you all week that the gorgeous Pastor Phillip McKnight would be on our show, and tonight is the night."

Serenity wanted to scream. She couldn't believe that she had just called Pastor McKnight gorgeous on camera for the world to hear. Her in-studio segment of the show was streaming live, so she couldn't take it back or edit it out if she wanted to. She just hoped and prayed that all of her viewers were running late to the show, especially Phillip. Maybe he was in a meeting or was too busy studying the Word of God to turn on her rinky-dink program.

"I was able to gain an exclusive interview with Pastor McKnight of New Destiny Church in Tampa, Florida, and we even filmed one of his sermons. I want you all to stay tuned the next three days, because you are in for the treat of a lifetime. So, let's get on with the show." Serenity sustained an enormous smile until the camera moved away from her, then lowered her head in shame.

Just then, Pam walked up to her. "Don't beat yourself up, Serenity. I caught your little slip, but that doesn't mean everybody else did."

Serenity lifted her head. "I practically called a pastor a hunk on live television, Pam. What's wrong with me?"

"Most of the women who watch our program may be saved, but they're not blind. Every last one of them will agree with you. And you've just given them permission to admit what their eyes can see, anyway," Pam said as she escorted Serenity off the set.

As they entered her office, Serenity asked, "Can you get someone to make some cue cards for the end of the program? I would hate to call the man gorgeous again while asking our viewers to purchase his ministry tapes and contribute to his building fund."

"Not a problem. I'll get on that right now. You just relax, and we'll see you back on the set in fifteen minutes."

Serenity sat down, put her head on her desk, and prayed, "Father, please help me."

Yes, she could admit it—Phillip McKnight was the most handsome man she had seen in a long time. And she was slightly attracted to him. But she had two really good reasons to get over any feelings she had for Phillip—first, he was a preacher, and, second, he was in no way attracted to her. When they'd first met, Serenity had thought he was trying to flirt with her, but he hadn't even been able to look her in the eye at her father's dinner party. And then, when they'd met at the studio, Phillip hadn't said anything to indicate any interest. *So, there. Get over it.*

Just then, the phone rang. She normally didn't take calls while the show was being aired, even if it was an already televised program. The only person who used to call during airtime on a regular basis was Michael. He'd never cared about anyone's time but his own. She picked up the phone, grateful for a distraction. "Serenity Williams speaking."

"If I had been a little bit more *gorgeous*, would you have interviewed *me* on your program?"

Why had she answered the phone? She should have expected it to be Michael. But she hadn't heard from him in months. How could she have known that he was still watching her show on a regular basis? "Why are you calling me in the middle of a show, Michael? I've asked you over and over not to do this."

"See, this is why I didn't marry you, Serenity—you're always too busy to talk to me. I need a wife who is on my time, not her own."

"You made that perfectly clear six months ago. Bye, Michael." She hung up the phone and gritted her teeth. To this day, she couldn't understand why she had fallen in love with such an egomaniac like Michael Randolph, but she thanked the Lord that He'd allowed Michael to break up with her, because she doubted she would have ended the relationship on her own. If she were married to that man right now, she'd be miserable. *Thank You, Jesus*.

She went back onstage and finished the show without any more embarrassing incidents, and she was thankful for that. As she walked off the set, Sandy came running over to her, carrying a bouquet of lilies in a crystal vase.

"These were just delivered for you," Sandy told her.

"Who sent them?" Serenity asked with a delighted smile. Lilies were her favorite flower.

"The card is right there," Sandy said as she handed off the vase.

Serenity thanked her and carried the flowers to her office. She inhaled their fragrance, placed them on the table, and sat down behind her desk, then opened the envelope to read the note.

It said, "Great show." Signed, "Gorgeous."

Six

SERENITY WAS ABSOLUTELY MORTIFIED. SHE RECEIVED calls from friends all around the country with this or that remark about how she'd called Phillip McKnight gorgeous on national television. But, on the upside, her uncharacteristic comment on the first day of the show was probably what caused the ratings to skyrocket the following two days. And Phillip received hundreds of thousands of dollars in donations to his building fund.

To show his gratitude, Phillip had sent two Visa gift cards, along with a note encouraging Serenity to give one to Lady Evelyn and paint the town wild on a mother-daughter shopping spree.

Pam's mouth dropped when Serenity showed her the gift cards. Most guests sent flowers, fruit baskets, or boxes of chocolate to express thanks after an interview, but no one had ever sent a Visa gift card. "He wants you to go on a shopping spree?"

"Don't get too excited, Pam. There's only fifty dollars on each of these cards."

"I don't think so, Serenity. He would look cheap if he did something like that. And what man, trying to impress a woman, wants to look cheap?"

"He isn't trying to impress me, Pam. I told him about the shopping trips that my mom and I used to take when I was a kid, and how we'd shop all day with just fifty bucks."

"You're talking about something you did in the eighties. You need to bring that brother up to the twenty-first century."

"I wish I could keep them," Serenity said, fingering the plastic cards. "It would have been fun to watch my mother hunt for bargains and haggle like she did when I was young."

"What do you mean, you wish you could keep them?"

"I don't feel right accepting money from a guest on the show," Serenity said, shaking her head.

"Girl, Phillip is the one who shouldn't feel right. That man is worth millions, and yet he sends you two fifty-dollar Visa cards. Please, keep them. You've received gifts of flowers and candy worth more than that from other preachers."

Pam was putting Phillip down because of the value of his gift, but Serenity actually thought it was sweet—endearing, even. The Visa gift cards meant more to her than any other gift she had ever received at the studio. Phillip had really listened, and he understood how much those days of shopping with her mother had meant to her. "I think I will keep them," she finally said, then went to her office to check her e-mail before calling it a day.

They had been receiving thousands of e-mails about the show, mostly from women asking for Phillip McKnight's telephone number. Serenity had laughed when she'd received the first such request, but by the time the fiftieth I-need-a-man e-mail came in, she really wanted to tell those women to stop chasing men and start chasing after God. She truly believed that if a person's mind was fixed on God, He would send the right mate into his or her life. She couldn't explain God's plans for her failed relationship with Michael, but she decided to trust that He had someone else for her, and, now, she needed to focus on her heavenly Father and keep Him first in her life.

One of the e-mails in her inbox had a subject line that read, "Open immediately." She didn't recognize the sender, and it sounded like it could be spam, so she didn't open it but rather viewed it through the preview window. The message was to the point: "Stay away from him. Don't make me hurt you."

What in the world? Why would someone send her a threatening e-mail like that? And who would want to hurt her? Serenity closed her e-mail, signed off from her computer, and grabbed her purse. As she walked out of the studio, she wondered about the identity of the person from whom she was supposed to stay away. She stopped in her tracks when she realized that the e-mail had to have been about Phillip. Although she had received plenty of calls and e-mails that joked about her calling Phillip gorgeous, someone obviously hadn't liked it. Serenity guessed that that someone was Michael. He probably thought that she had moved on, was angry, and wanted to scare her. What a jerk.

Putting the matter out of her mind, Serenity got into her car, pulled out her cell phone, and called her mother. "Hey, Serenity," she said when she picked up. "I just finished watching the show. I think the third day was the best. You and your crew did such a great job of bringing Phillip's mission and his ministry into light, I even sent in a donation for the building fund!"

"Thanks, Mom. And Phillip just sent something here for you."

The surprise in her mother's voice was evident when she replied, "For me? He called here the other day and asked about your favorite flower, but I thought he was going to send lilies to the studio to thank you."

"He did. I'd wondered how he'd known to send lilies."

"Well, I certainly didn't expect him to send *me* a gift." Serenity giggled. "I told him about the fifty-dollar shopping sprees we used to go on when I was a kid, so he sent us a couple of fifty-dollar gift cards. What do you think? Do you still have it in you?"

"Oh, now, don't you get to thinking that I've lost my touch because your father earns a decent salary. I can still find a great bargain with the best of them."

"How about it, then? Tomorrow's Saturday. Would you like to spend it shopping with your daughter, for old times' sake?" As Serenity had grown older, and life had become more hectic, she and her mother had let their Saturday shopping sprees fall by the wayside.

"I would love to spend the day with you, Serenity. It's been so long since we've gone on one of our shopping sprees. I'm so excited! Plus, we get to spend someone else's money. How much better could life be?"

∽

The next morning, Serenity picked up her mother and drove straight to McDonald's for breakfast before beginning their bargain hunt. "You know I love McDonald's breakfast," her mother said as they waited in line for their orders to be filled, "but why aren't we at your favorite breakfast place?"

"Because we'll spend a lot less here than at the Marriott's breakfast buffet," Serenity explained, picking up her tray and heading toward a table.

"Honey, I gladly would have treated you to breakfast at the Marriott."

"It's not about the money, Mom. I think Phillip sent us those gift cards as a challenge."

"What do you mean?"

"I don't think he believes that we can shop all day and spend less than fifty bucks apiece. So, I'm going to show him just how frugal the Williams women can be."

"Have you thanked Phillip for the gift cards?"

"Not yet. I'm going to e-mail him a thank-you note, along with some pictures from our shopping spree to prove that we stayed within our budget."

"That's my girl. I wouldn't want him to think you have no home training."

"Oh, I've got home training," Serenity said, "and this little baby is going to help me prove it." She pulled out her digital camera. "Smile!" she said, then snapped a picture of her mother holding up her Bacon, Egg & Cheese McGriddle.

"He really doesn't believe that we're able to find good bargains?" her mother asked, setting her breakfast tray back on the table.

"He practically accused me of lying when I told him about our fifty-dollar shopping sprees. Trust me, Mom, the man is testing us." What she couldn't explain was why.

"Well, I love him to pieces for doing this for us. Michael certainly never would have. That man couldn't stand for you to spend time with anyone other than him."

"Michael has issues. Do you know he had the nerve to call me this week?"

"What? Don't tell me he's finally come to his senses."

"Oh, please. He was upset that I called Phillip gorgeous, and he basically accused me of not bringing him on the show because I thought he wasn't handsome enough."

Her mother laughed out loud.

"It's not funny, Mom. Michael is very handsome. He has a growing ministry, and he had someone who loved him, but nothing is ever good enough for that man."

Her mother patted Serenity's hand. "Preachers aren't Jesus, Himself; some of them need deliverance, too. But I'm so glad you didn't marry Michael. I just don't think he would have made you happy."

"Enough about Michael," Serenity said, ready to change the subject. "Guess who's pregnant?"

Her mother clapped her hands together as joy lit her face. "It's Melinda, isn't it?"

"Can you believe it? Melinda is so excited. She says that Brianna can't wait to be a big sister, either."

"I'm so happy for Melinda and Steven. Maybe, one day, one of my children will give me some grandchildren. At the rate Larry and Jay are going, I don't think they'll ever get married, and Monroe can't stop planning his next campaign long enough to think about being a father."

"If you ask me, Monroe needs to worry more about being a good husband right now. Cathy seems so un-happy."

Her mother frowned. "I know. I've been praying for those two. Monroe really needs to get it together." She paused, then eyed Serenity. "And what about you, young lady? Do you think you could talk Phillip into marrying you so I can have some grandchildren?"

"On that note," Serenity said, standing up, "let's go shopping."

⁓

What am I doing? Phillip wondered. He had been watching Serenity's show all week long and was growing more and more infatuated with every episode. She was beautiful, yes, but it wasn't her outward looks that had caused him to sit, transfixed, in front of the television. After all, Chantel had been beautiful when he'd met her and just as beautiful when she'd ripped his heart out. It was Serenity's propensity for saving money that had piqued his interest, and her heart for ministry had attracted him further. So far, he knew that she liked nice things but was wise with the way she spent her money. As much as he hated to admit it, he had sent her those Visa cards to see how she spent other people's money. Would she consider him cheap? Call him up and complain, wondering what he expected her to be able to buy with only fifty dollars? Or would she rise to the challenge? This was Phillip's gold digger test, and he hoped and prayed that Serenity would pass it.

The phone rang, and Phillip looked at the caller ID. It was Chantel. She had been calling and leaving messages for the past several days, but Phillip hadn't returned her calls. *Might as well get it over with*, he thought as he picked up the phone. "Hey, Chantel. What's up?"

"How are you doing, Phillip?"

"I'm making it. How about yourself?"

"You know me. I'm always going to rise to the top," Chantel said, as if she was the ruler of her own destiny.

Why hadn't he noticed how arrogant she was when he'd been falling all over himself asking her to marry him? "Is there something you need, Chantel?"

"I was just trying to warn you about what my lawyer is up to."

"What are you talking about?"

"My lawyer saw the show you did on *Walk This Way* with Serenity Williams."

"And?"

"And, you know how Peter is." Chantel sounded almost bored as she continued. "He thinks that you withheld the knowledge of this little fund-raiser until the divorce was final so you wouldn't have to submit those funds as income."

"Well, then, your lawyer is way off base, because we sold my ministry tapes to raise money for missions."

"Yeah, but don't most preachers receive money from the ministry tapes they sell? What part of the fund-raiser was your income, and what part went to the church?"

Phillip closed his eyes for a second and exhaled, wondering if he'd ever be free from this money-grubbing woman. "I didn't earn a dime from that fund-raiser. It's all going toward building the church."

Venom was in her voice now. "Why are you so obsessed with building that church? You could have done it cheaper. Could have asked your members for more money so that you didn't have to cut into our money."

"Did you need anything else, Chantel?"

"What if we'd had children, Phillip? Would you still have thrown away our money like that?"

She was touching on a sore spot, but she'd never cared how she'd hurt him. All he'd ever wanted was a family, and he had begged Chantel to have his baby. But, year after year, she'd kept saying that it wasn't the right time. She had been worried about stretch marks and weight gain. He'd been attracted to Chantel because of her beauty. Somehow, he'd allowed her looks to blind him to the truth about her personality. They'd gotten married five years before he gave his life to Christ, an experience that opened his eyes to the truth—including the truth about Chantel. "We don't have children, Chantel, so I don't even have to consider that, do I?"

"You're cruel, Phillip."

"I have to go, Chantel. Please have your lawyer contact my lawyer if you think of anything else that needs to be discussed." With that, Phillip hung up, then went into his home office to check his e-mail.

He turned on his computer and tapped his finger on his desk while waiting for it to boot up. He was so angry with himself for being stupid. His one saving grace was that he didn't fall all over himself for pretty women anymore. Instead, he avoided them like the plague. Women had always thrown themselves at him, but he'd given up caring. That is, until Serenity had walked through his door. But he would be no good for Serenity because his ex-wife had really messed him up. He knew he needed to forgive Chantel in order to move on, but forgiveness was hard sometimes, even for preachers.

In the next few minutes, Phillip responded to a few e-mails he'd read earlier. He also sent a message to his divorce lawyer, giving him a heads-up about Chantel seeking more money. He had been online for about thirty minutes when an e-mail from Serenity popped up in his inbox. The subject line read, "Thanks for the gift cards."

He opened Serenity's e-mail and began reading.

Phillip,

First, let me thank you not just for thinking about me, but for including my mother in the gift, too. You've gained a friend for life in Evelyn Williams. We had a wonderful day. My mom and I hadn't had a secondhand shopping spree since I began *Walk This Way*. Let's just say that she and I needed to spend some quality time together. I am forever in your debt.

Sincerely,
Serenity

PS: I have a suspicion that you sent those cards as a challenge, because you probably think that my mom and I have lost our bargain-hunting skills after all these years. Therefore, I have included the attached pictures to provide a detailed summary of how we spent our money. By the way, I still have three dollars left on my gift card, so I'll have to take you to lunch the next time you're in town. ☺

He was smiling uncontrollably as he read Serenity's words. When he'd almost memorized what she'd written, he clicked on the first picture and saw Serenity and Lady Evelyn having breakfast at McDonald's. In the next picture, Serenity was standing at the front counter of a store with a clerk, holding up a pair of off-white linen pants and a blue jean jacket. Then, he clicked on another photo, which showed Lady Evelyn paying for a pair of brown pumps and a yellow and blue silk scarf.

From the photographs, Phillip could tell that the Williams women weren't just picking up junk in order to avoid exceeding the card balances. They really knew how to shop for quality stuff. The final picture displayed receipts from the stores where they had shopped. He couldn't make out the totals on all of the receipts, but he was sure that Serenity would be willing to produce them in person. The final item in Serenity's e-mail was a video clip of Lady Evelyn haggling with a clerk. He was impressed.

He typed out a response to Serenity's e-mail that said, "Okay, you've made a believer out of me. You are the man!"

Phillip had no game plan in mind for his next move with Serenity. As a professional football player, he'd had a reason for every move he'd made on the football field. But in the game of his personal life, Phillip didn't have a clue what came next. However, after viewing those pictures of Serenity on her so-called shopping spree, he found that he wanted to get to know this woman in ways he hadn't wanted to know another woman since Chantel had left him. But he knew that he wouldn't be able to move forward until he could put the past behind him. So, he turned off his computer, opened his Bible, and began reviewing what the Word of God had to say about forgiveness.

Seven

TURN IN YOUR BIBLES TO THE BOOK OF MATTHEW, chapter five," Phillip said, standing before his congregation. "Let's start reading verses forty-three and forty-four: *'You have heard that it was said, "You shall love your neighbor and hate your enemy." But I say to you, love your enemies, bless those who curse you, do good to those who hate you, and pray for those who spitefully use you and persecute you.'* And then, verse forty-six: *'For if you love those who love you, what reward have you? Do not even the tax collectors do the same?'*

"A lot of you are nodding, as if you agree with these verses. But let's put these words into action. Let's say an enemy approaches you, and, instead of apologizing for what he's done to you, he offends you again. You'd feel pretty justified in hating him, wouldn't you?

"Or what if some of you ladies are out on a daylong shopping spree, and you find the perfect blouse? It's the right color, the right size, and it goes with an outfit you've had in your closet for months, just waiting on this particular blouse. And then, just as you are getting ready to take it off the rack, some other woman grabs it and runs to the register with it. Now, do you forgive her, or will you hold a grudge forever?"

When the service was over, Phillip went into his office, grabbed a Pepsi out of the fridge, loosened his tie, and sat down on his couch.

"What was that all about?" asked Elder Derek Mann as he walked into Phillip's office.

Phillip set his Pepsi bottle on the coffee table. "What are you talking about?"

"I haven't heard you use a shopping analogy since Chantel left. I hope you haven't found another woman to run up your charge cards."

"Hardly," Phillip said, as he thought about the fifty dollars he'd given Serenity and her mother to spend.

"So, what gives?"

The two men had been friends for over a decade. Phillip had first met Derek when he'd been traded to the Tampa Bay Buccaneers. Derek had already been on the team for five years, but they had become the best of friends within six months. It was Derek who had invited Phillip to church the night he'd given his life to Christ. And, when Phillip had accepted the call to be a pastor, he had asked Derek to help him build the ministry. Derek knew him. He wouldn't be able to hide his feelings for much longer. "Do you remember Serenity Williams?"

"The talk show host who interviewed you a few weeks ago? Yeah, I know who you're talking about."

"I've seen her a couple times since she interviewed me."

"You're dating her?"

Phillip shook his head. "She came to the dinner her father gave for me when I met with him, and then I went to her studio to review the edited version of the show."

Derek shrugged. "Okay...?"

"She's—uh, got sort of a shopping habit."

"Now, we're getting somewhere! I thought you were going to stay away from those high-maintenance, spend-somebody-else's-money women."

"Serenity's not like that. She grew up going on 'shopping sprees' in thrift stores with her mother, and the most they would spend in one day was fifty dollars. She's really very good with money."

"I hope it doesn't rain anytime soon, because this woman has your nose wide open. And you'd better hope Chantel doesn't find out about this obsession you have." With that, Derek turned and walked out the door, laughing to himself.

As far as Phillip was concerned, there was nothing funny about his predicament. That shopping analogy hadn't even been in his notes. That meant Serenity was in his head, even when he was supposed to be delivering his sermon. God help him.

∽

That weekend, Serenity was the guest speaker at a Women in Ministry conference in Nashville, Tennessee. Standing behind the podium before thousands of conference attendees, she said, "Turn with me to the book of Matthew, chapter seven, starting with verse seven," then began to read aloud. *"Ask, and it will be given to you; seek, and you will find; knock, and it will be opened to you. For everyone who asks receives, and he who seeks finds, and to him who knocks it will be opened. Or what man is there among you who, if his son asks for bread, will give him a stone? Or if he asks for a fish, will he give him a serpent?'*

"Now, I know some of you are about ready to ask for a time-out or a review of the play, because even though this parable indicates that God has our backs, we don't always feel as if that's true. In fact, to relate this particular parable to a football game, it's similar to a quarterback counting on the fullback and the left and right guards to protect him. But, if we're quarterbacks, we often feel as if our own guards are throwing us down in the dirt instead of protecting us from the opposing team. Sometimes, things happen to us that break us down so bad that we find ourselves wondering if God is truly listening. Can we really ask and receive from Him? Can we trust Him to be our guard? To quote President Obama, 'Yes, we can.'"

Serenity continued with her sermon, encouraging the listeners to trust God with their ministries, their lives, and their love. To conclude her message, Serenity closed her Bible and gave an altar call for any women having trouble getting their ministries off the ground or in need of encouragement to keep on believing that God would answer their prayers. The altar area filled up quickly.

When Serenity finished, she walked to the back and took a seat in the room reserved for the speakers. Serenity didn't like to mingle among the attendees after giving a sermon. Often, she was worn out and needed to rest before she could think clearly again. She stretched out on the couch and closed her eyes.

The door opened, and Melinda Marks came into the room, carrying a sandwich. "Hey, girl. Are you too good to mingle with us lowly workers in the kingdom?"

Serenity sat up and smiled at her friend. Melinda was one of the speakers at the conference, too, which was one of the reasons Serenity had signed up for this particular conference. She needed to see her best friend in the worst way. "Not everyone has the energy that you have, Melinda. Preaching knocks the wind out of me. And you know that I'm not much of a mingler."

Melinda handed her the sandwich. "Here, eat."

Serenity smiled as she took the sandwich from Melinda, thankful that her friend knew her well. She rarely ate before she delivered a sermon. Fasting was her way of sacrificing for the people to whom she would minister. During her fasts, she would pray that God would work through her to speak life and bring hope to those who desperately needed it.

Melinda sat down next to Serenity. "No, you've never been much for mingling, but you certainly seem to be a football expert all of a sudden. What were all those football analogies about?"

Serenity took a bite of her sandwich, chewed and swallowed, and then said, "I haven't the slightest idea what you're talking about, Melinda Marks. The football terms fit with my message, that's all; nothing more to it."

"Most of the people in the auditorium were scratching their heads, wondering what you were talking about. Admit it, Serenity—a football game is one of the worst analogies you can use to illustrate a point to a bunch of women."

When Serenity didn't respond, Melinda said, "Your message was about asking and receiving from God. You wouldn't be asking God for a certain football player-turned-preacher, whom we both know as 'Gorgeous,' now, would you?"

Serenity put her head on Melinda's shoulder and whimpered. "I can't get him out of my head, Melinda. What am I going to do?"

"I don't see why you're so upset about it. From what you've told me about Phillip, he seems like a really nice guy."

"It would never work between us."

"Why?"

Serenity lifted her head off Melinda's shoulder and gave her an "Isn't it obvious?" look. "He's a preacher. And, other than your father and mine, I can't name one single male preacher who doesn't have a head the size of Mount Rushmore."

"That's not a fair statement, Serenity. The simple label of *preacher* does not automatically determine that a person will be prideful or egotistical. There are plenty of good men out there who also happen to be pastors."

"Yeah? Name some."

"My husband, for one. Steven is a good man. He treats his family and his congregation the way a man of God should. He always considers us before himself."

"Well, you didn't feel that way before you married him. Steven didn't even believe that women should preach. Now, that's egotistical, if you ask me."

"No one is perfect, Serenity. And Yvonne Milner's husband, David, didn't believe that women should preach, either, but he came around. Men and women may not agree on every issue, but that doesn't make either of them evil."

Serenity gasped, horrified to realize she had just criticized Melinda's husband. In the handbook of friendship, that was a big no-no. "I'm so sorry, Melinda. I shouldn't have said that about Steven. You're right—he is a good man. I'm just upset with myself because I keep thinking about Phillip."

"Look, Serenity. I know you got the short end of the stick with Michael. But that doesn't mean all preachers are as insecure and ego-driven as he is."

"But how can I be sure of that, Melinda? Do you know how much it hurts to give your heart to someone and then have him tell you that your love isn't good enough?" A tear rolled down her cheek, but she quickly wiped it away. "I remember how angry Michael used to get when we'd go out to dinner and someone would recognize me from my television program but wouldn't know who he was. I should have known right then that he had issues. I mean, how can you be upset with someone about a ministry that God is prospering?"

"Look on the bright side," Melinda said with a smile. "You wouldn't have that problem with Phillip. He's known all over the country. The man was on TV just about every Sunday during his NFL career."

"You're right about that. Phillip is so well-known that having him on my show doubled my ratings."

"Well, see? There you go. You won't have to worry about Phillip being jealous of your popularity."

"Yeah, but that man has other issues. That ex-wife of his really did a number on him. I can see the sadness in his eyes. I can't fix something like that, Melinda."

"It's not your job to fix it." Melinda put a hand on Serenity's shoulder. "You know that I had some issues to deal with a couple of years ago. Steven and I wanted to be together, but I couldn't be a part of his life—or Brianna's—until God dealt with me. So, if you think Phillip has some issues to deal with, my only suggestion to you, dear friend, is not to fall too fast. Let God do the work in him that needs to be done."

"You're right. I don't need the distraction, anyway. I got my first hate mail after we did those segments with Phillip."

"You didn't tell me anything about that. What happened?"

"I normally receive a bunch of e-mails after I do guest interviews, but they've almost always been supportive—people commenting on how the interviewee helped them deal with some issue he or she had been struggling with, kind of like the way Yvonne Milner's interview helped Steven to change his mind on women preachers. But this one was different."

"What did it say?"

"It said, 'Stay away from him. Don't make me hurt you.'"

"Did you call the police?" Melinda asked.

"No."

"Why wouldn't you call the police, Serenity?"

"I received only one e-mail. It was probably a prank."

Melinda shook her head. "You can't be so cavalier about things like this. You're a public figure. People can view you on television five times a week. And some of them might be a little unstable."

"It might just be Michael. He was upset about the interview I did with Phillip, so he's probably trying to spook me."

"Or, it might be a crazy person you don't know. Serenity, you can't take this stuff too lightly. As I said before, this guy might be unstable and dangerous."

"You're right about that," Serenity agreed. "I remember reading about this woman who thought she was married to David Letterman and said that he was sending her messages through the television set. She eventually killed herself."

"See what I mean? You've got to protect yourself from crazy people," Melinda said. "Call the police, or I'm going to call your mother."

⁓

A month later, Serenity was still laughing at Melinda's threat to call her mother, as if she were a wayward child disobeying a babysitter. Serenity was still convinced that Michael had sent her that e-mail because he was hurt that she'd moved on. And, even if it hadn't been Michael, she hadn't received another e-mail like it, so the sender had probably gotten over being angry.

But Melinda had been right about one thing. Serenity had no time for a man in need of deliverance, especially when she'd already been there and done that. Granted, Phillip's deliverance had nothing to do with his being prideful. But, as far as Serenity was concerned, a man with a broken heart was just as dangerous as a man with a swollen head. So, she concentrated on her ministry and tried her best to put Phillip McKnight out of her mind.

But that was easier said than done, especially since she had accepted an invitation to speak at an event in Tampa, Florida, and would be there next week. Serenity kept picking up the telephone to call Phillip to invite him to dinner after her speaking engagement, but she didn't have the nerve to ask a man out. Her mother's maxim kept screaming at her: *"Women never throw themselves at men."*

Besides, what would she actually gain by letting Phillip know that she would be in Tampa? She had visited the city before and had never felt compelled to call Phillip McKnight. However, she hadn't known him personally during those other visits. The man had eaten dinner with her family, increased her show's ratings, and sent her on a shopping spree, after all. Didn't she owe him a call out of courtesy?

Eight

PHILLIP COULDN'T GET SERENITY OUT OF HIS MIND. The emotions he'd been feeling recently were strange to him, especially since he had determined never to fall in love again. He had no desire to be in another one-sided relationship. But Serenity was different. She didn't seem like the type of woman who plotted and schemed to get a man to fall in love with her just so she could break his heart. Still, he had to be careful. Though he didn't want to admit it, as a man, he wanted to appear strong no matter what, but, in truth, his heart was fragile right now.

That was why he had hopped a plane to Chicago and was now sitting with Bishop Williams in his home office. Phillip figured that if he told the Bishop how he was damaged goods, the man would help steer him clear away from his one and only daughter. "I know that we haven't been working together that long," Phillip began, "but I respect and admire you, so I really need to tell you what's going on with me."

Bishop Williams stood up from the chair behind his desk, unbuttoned his jacket, and came around to the other side, where he took the seat next to Phillip. "What's on your mind, son?"

Phillip lowered his head, trying to think of the best way to tell Bishop Williams about his feelings for Serenity.

When he looked up again, he noticed that the Bishop was holding his breath. He figured he'd better spit it out before he caused the man to pass out. "I can't stop thinking about your daughter."

"What?" Bishop Williams said, letting out a whoosh of air.

"I haven't been able to get Serenity off my mind, sir. And, believe me, I've tried. But from the moment I met Serenity, I've been on an emotional roller coaster."

Bishop Williams started laughing, then slapped his knee. "I knew there was something to that 'Take your mother on a shopping spree' scheme of yours."

Phillip lifted his hands in protest. "To be honest, sir, I wasn't sure I wanted to be with Serenity when I sent those gift cards. I mean, come on—what man tries to impress a woman with a fifty-dollar gift card?"

"It wasn't the amount; it was the sentiment that sent my wife to the moon and back. She hasn't stopped talking about it. As a matter of fact, she told Larry that he could take a few pointers from you on how to woo a woman." He stood up, shaking his head and grinning. "You scared me for a minute there. I thought you were going to confess to something that we'd have to call in our attorneys for."

"Is that why you were holding your breath?"

"Holding it and praying silently. When you've been a bishop as long as I have, you find out pretty quickly that some pastors are wolves in sheep's clothing."

"I hope never to be that, sir. I just want to serve the Lord and do the best job I can for my congregation."

Bishop Williams gave Phillip a pat on the shoulder. "I know you do. That's why I agreed to preside over your church."

"Okay, but how do you feel about what I just said about Serenity?" Now it was Phillip's turn to hold his breath.

"Given what you told me about your previous marriage, I guess I'd like to know how *you* feel about what you told me," Bishop Williams said.

Phillip wished he hadn't been so brutally honest during his initial meeting with Bishop Williams. When the man had asked Phillip what he thought of marriage, in light of his recent divorce, he had blurted out, "Marriage isn't for me. I tried it once, and that turned out to be the biggest mistake of my life. I'd rather just live my life for Jesus and let that be that."

"I know what I said about marriage; I also know that I still feel betrayed and bitter about the whole thing. But Serenity is nothing like my ex-wife."

"Yes, but have you gotten over your ex-wife?"

"I don't want her back, if that's what you mean."

"That's not what I mean, at all. Will you measure every woman you meet by your ex-wife, thereby making other women pay for what she did to you?"

Phillip wanted to say no. Of course not. He had enough sense to realize that Chantel, and no one else, had wronged him. But then he remembered his reaction at seeing that Gucci watch on Serenity's wrist. He'd wanted nothing to do with Serenity until he'd realized how frugal she really was. So, hadn't he been making her pay for what Chantel had done to him? "Chantel really messed me up, sir. I've been trying to forgive her, but it's been the hardest thing I've ever had to do."

"Then, do yourself—and Serenity—a favor, son. Get closure on the old relationship before you begin a new one."

∽

Before speaking with Bishop Williams, Phillip had told Lady Evelyn that he would stop by the studio to see Serenity while he was in Chicago. But after the conversation, he felt compelled to rush back to Tampa to see Chantel. He'd called her en route, and she had assured him that she would leave the door open. That was another thing that galled him. He'd lived in the house for five years before he'd married Chantel, but she'd gotten to keep it after the divorce settlement. So, now, he had to knock on his own door—unless, of course, she left the door unlocked. How kind of her. *Not.*

Stop thinking these thoughts, Phillip ordered himself as he stood in the foyer, waiting for Chantel. *You've got to find a way to forgive this woman.* She kept him waiting for ten minutes. When she finally appeared at the top of the spiral staircase, she was wearing a cream-colored, form-fitting dress she'd bought after seeing it on the runway at a fashion show in Paris. Phillip had liked the dress better on the runway model.

"I hope I didn't keep you waiting too long," Chantel said, slowly descending the stairs.

"I've done nothing but wait for you since the day we met. Why should I stop now, just because of a little thing like a divorce?" *Cool it*, he told himself, then remembered Proverbs 16:32: *"He who is slow to anger is better than the mighty, and he who rules his spirit than he who takes a city."*

Chantel sauntered over to Phillip and pinched his cheek. He stepped back, out of her reach. "Don't be bitter, baby," she crooned. "That's not a good look on you."

"Can we sit down and talk?"

"I hope you're not here to beg me to take you back again, because I'm not ready for that kind of commitment right now."

Phillip held his tongue as anger boiled inside him. The woman stepped on his heart every chance she got, but the last time he'd set foot inside this house had been

one month before the divorce was final. He had been
there to beg her to take him back, and she'd laughed in
his face, had even gone so far as to ask him, "Do you really think you're worth ten million dollars? I mean, you're
cute, but you're not *that* cute."

"Don't worry, Chantel. I'll never ask you to come back
to me again." He was over her—that was one thing Phillip
knew for sure. But he also knew that he was still bitter
over the way things had ended between them. He needed
to find a way to forgive this woman so that he could move
on with his life. "I just need to talk to you."

"Follow me, then," she said, turning on her heels and
strutting down the hall toward the family room. Phillip
noticed that the comfortable sleeper sofa sectional he had
purchased for the family room was gone. In its place were
four chocolate-colored chaise lounges, which looked like
something out of *The Jetsons*.

"I see you've done some redecorating,"

"Yes," Chantel said as she plopped down onto one of
the lounge chairs. "That other stuff just wasn't my style."

Phillip sat down on the chaise lounge next to hers
and tried to get situated, but the chair was very uncomfortable. Finally, he just stood back up, figuring Chantel
had purchased these chairs so that guests wouldn't stay
too long. *Mission accomplished*, he thought. He certainly
didn't want to be there any longer than he needed to. "I
came here because I needed to ask you something."

"Shoot."

"I need to know why you married me."

Her forehead crinkled in confusion, and she sat up. "I
don't understand the question, Phillip."

"I asked you to marry me because I had fallen in love
with you. I thought you loved me, too, but I just don't
know how I could have missed your real motivation."

"And what was my motivation, Phillip?" she asked, her hands on her hips.

"Money."

Chantel stood up and walked over to him with fire in her eyes. "You can think what you want about my reason for divorcing you. But you've got my reason for marrying you all wrong."

"You don't have to lie to me now, Chantel."

"Do you think you were the only rich guy with money trying to get next to me?" She stepped back and posed so that Phillip could see every inch of her attractive figure. "I had plenty of offers."

"Then, why'd you pick me?"

"Because I loved you, stupid. Why do you think?"

Phillip shook his head, trying to clear away some of the fog. He didn't understand this woman, and he wasn't sure his visit was going to help much in that regard. He decided to ask another question, anyway. "If you loved me, why weren't you interested in trying to work things out? Why did you cheat on me?"

"Chad didn't mean anything to me; I was just passing time with him. He actually took me out; he bought me nice things."

"Okay, but then you dumped him, and you divorced me without going to counseling or anything."

Chantel collapsed into her chaise lounge again. "Look, Phillip. It was nothing personal. But, when I was a little girl, my mother held down three jobs, and we still lived in the ghetto. I promised myself that I would never live in poverty another day of my life."

"We were far from poverty, Chantel."

"But you were throwing all our money away. And, although I see now that you can earn a very nice living as a pastor, you really had no idea whether you would earn back the money you put toward building that church." She shook her head. "If I hadn't divorced you and taken my half when I did, I have no doubt that you would have spent all of our money. And I don't look good in hand-me-downs."

She might not look good in hand-me-downs, but Phillip knew who did. "Thanks for being honest with me, Chantel. I'll see you around." He turned and started walking toward the front entryway.

"Wait," Chantel said, getting up and coming after him. "What was all this about, Phillip? Why do you suddenly care why I married you?"

He stopped at the front door and turned to face her. "I need closure, Chantel. I can't carry this bitterness around with me anymore."

"But when we divorced, you told me that you'd never get over what I did to you. What's changed?"

Phillip didn't respond. He put his hand on the door-knob.

Chantel gasped with a look of comprehension. "There's someone else, isn't there?"

"In my heart? You better believe there is," Phillip said. With that, he opened the door and walked away from Chantel, feeling lighter on his feet than he had in years.

Nine

SERENITY HAD BEEN AGONIZING OVER HER UPCOMING trip to Tampa. She thought it would be rude to visit Phillip's town without saying hello, so she made a decision. She would simply stop by Phillip's church to check on the progress they'd made on the building. That wasn't too forward at all—just one friend checking on another. But then, her mother called and wrecked that idea.

"Hey, hon! Did you get a chance to see Phillip yesterday?" her mother asked her.

"Was he on TV or something?" Serenity asked, looking in the mirror as she wiped off her stage makeup.

"No, Phillip had a meeting with your father yesterday. He told me that he might stop by the studio to see you before he left town. Maybe he was running late and couldn't fit everything into his schedule. Just forget I mentioned it."

But how was Serenity just supposed to forget something like that? Phillip had been in her town, and he hadn't been able to take ten minutes out of his day to say hello to her? His actions spoke volumes, as far as Serenity was concerned. Well, if he didn't want to be bothered with her, she certainly wasn't going to waste her time stopping by New Destiny Church. She would go to Tampa, deliver her sermon, and fly right back home the next afternoon without saying a single word to Phillip.

However, at the conference, when she was escorted to her seat behind the podium, Serenity noticed that Phillip was among the pastors and preachers already sitting there. Phillip smiled at her, and she smiled back, trying not to look surprised, then sat down in the seat reserved for the speaker. This women's conference was being filmed live for Daystar, and Serenity didn't want to appear flustered at seeing Phillip. She wasn't, of course—why would she be? He was just a man, like any other.

Serenity prayed that the Lord would guide her tongue and keep her mind off of Phillip as she delivered her sermon. When she stood up at the podium, she smiled at the crowd and said, "Praise the Lord, from whom all blessings flow. Well, I just came to exhort you tonight. See, somebody told me that you all really love the Lord and desire to do His will." The crowd stood up and clapped. When the applause subsided, she went on, "I came to deliver a word to you, and it is simply that no matter what obstacles you have to deal with this year, no matter who has caused you to think less of yourself, God is still on your side."

Serenity led the people of God in prayer and then preached for an hour and ten minutes concerning the goodness of God and His ability to put His chosen people right where they are supposed to be. The topic meant a lot to Serenity, who understood that she truly had been blessed by God. Her ministry was flourishing and helping countless people, as evidenced by the e-mails and phone calls she received. She wanted others to experience the joy of seeing their dreams come true. Her choice in ministry had cost her Michael, who seemed to believe that she'd decided to get into television ministry in order to show him up. He'd gotten upset when people recognized her in public but didn't know who he was. Michael had the love and adoration of his entire congregation but begrudged her a few casual hellos. Meanwhile, he didn't seem to value the relationships he had cultivated with his church members as much as he craved the impersonal hellos Serenity received from strangers on the street. She was far from envious, though—in her eyes, the fewer intimate ties one formed, the better.

Serenity had her reasons. She'd seen her mother cry and her father worry over members who'd once professed undying love for them and their ministry but had later spit in their faces with accusations and cruel remarks. She had seen it occur so many times that she had known, even before she'd graduated from Bible college, that she would never pastor a church.

Her brother Larry had seen the same heartbreaking things that she'd seen, but he'd decided to pastor a church, anyway. After Larry's second year as pastor, one of his elders had started his own church and taken half of Larry's church members with him. The whole thing had been quite messy, and, even though Larry had been able to rebuild and was still going strong, Serenity didn't have the stomach for dealing with that kind of drama.

By the time she finished her sermon, she was exhausted and in need of a back-room escape. But Phillip didn't let her run and hide. "Serenity!" he said, catching up with her afterward. "I enjoyed your sermon. Your brother told me that the anointing flows out of your pores when you preach. This was my first time witnessing it in person, but I've got to say, he was right."

"Thank you," Serenity said.

"So, what are you doing for dinner?"

Serenity looked around, trying to see if any of the preachers on the stage were watching them. Seeing that they all appeared to be involved in their own conversations, she turned back to Phillip. "I was going to grab something and take it to my hotel room."

"No way. Your father would kick me out of the fellowship if I let you eat alone. Come on, I'm taking you out to dinner, and it won't be McDonald's."

Serenity couldn't help laughing. She never should have shown Phillip that picture of her mother and her eating breakfast at the Golden Arches. During her teenage years, her father had constantly told her, "Never let a man treat you like a cheap date." But this wasn't really a date, according to Phillip; he was taking her out because her father would expect it. She was still smarting from the fact that Phillip had been in Chicago last week and hadn't stopped by to see her, though. So, she said, "Please, don't worry about it. I'm sure you have better things to do than spend time with me."

The conference host came up to them and gave Serenity a hug. "You were awesome, Serenity."

"Thank you for inviting me, Barbara," Serenity said as they broke their embrace.

"No, thank *you* for accepting my invitation to preach. The ladies won't soon forget this night."

Serenity smiled. "My prayer is that the Lord really opened their hearts and spirits to receive all that He has for them."

"Amen to that," Barbara said, then turned to Phillip. "So, are you all set?"

"She's trying to weasel out on me, but I'm not taking no for an answer."

Barbara turned back to Serenity and asked, "Do you like Italian food?"

"Love it," Serenity admitted.

"Then I wouldn't turn down this meal. Phillip has reservations at Armani's, one of the best Italian restaurants in the Tampa area," she said with a wink. Then, she walked away to greet another group of people.

"You got reservations before knowing whether or not I would want to go to dinner with you?" Serenity asked, raising her eyebrows.

Phillip lowered his voice. "Your father told me that you don't like crowded events, and I knew that Barbara was planning to take you to dinner with all the committee members, so I told her I already had it covered."

"I don't understand why you would want to take me to dinner when you didn't even bother to say hello to me while you were in Chicago last week." There. She'd said it. And even though she could hear the pitiful whine in each word, she couldn't help herself. She needed to know why he had blown her off last week and had made dinner reservations for two tonight. Was this simply about impressing her father, or something more?

"I wanted to see you, Serenity, but I had to take an earlier flight back to Tampa to take care of an urgent matter."

"Oh," was all she said, and then she quickly closed her mouth for fear that if she left it open too long, more bitter words might seep out.

"Are you ready?" Phillip asked.

Well, she was hungry. "All right, let's go." Serenity followed Phillip out to his car. When they started driving, she said, "You were mighty confident that I would agree to go to dinner with you. What if I hadn't been hungry? What would you have done with that reservation?"

"Your dad told me that you fast before most of your speaking engagements, so I figured it was a safe bet that you'd be hungry," Phillip said with a grin on his face.

"My father seems to be telling a lot of my business lately. I might need to have a little chat with him."

"No worries, Serenity. I come in peace. You have nothing to fear from me. Even if I knew all your secrets, I wouldn't tell a soul."

"That's what you say now. But if a tabloid offered you enough money, you'd sing like a bird."

"Never, ever would I betray your trust." He took his eyes off the road for a moment to look at her, then said, "But if you're really worried, I could always tell you a few of my secrets. That way, you could earn a little money from the tabloids, too."

Secrets from a two-time Super Bowl champion would certainly be juicier than any secrets of Serenity's, but she could never betray someone's confidence like that. She couldn't throw away someone's hard-earned trust. And Serenity freely admitted to herself that she had issues with trust because of all the people she'd witnessed change their minds or fail to keep their words.

"What did I say? You got quiet all of a sudden."

Serenity turned to Phillip. He seemed like a really nice guy, but she realized she didn't know much about him. "I was just thinking about trust, and how people do things to destroy it."

Phillip pulled the car in front of a valet station. "We're here."

They got out of the car, entered the Grand Hyatt, and took the elevator to the top level, where Armani's was located. The floor-to-ceiling windows, with their panoramic view of Tampa Bay, took Serenity's breath away.

The maître d' seated them at a table overlooking the city skyline. It was stunning, and the fading light of evening made the look and feel of everything that much more appealing. Serenity leaned closer to Phillip and whispered, "Do you hear a piano playing?"

"They have a pianist in the lounge. We can go over there after dinner, if you'd like."

"Oh," Serenity said, wondering why Phillip would bring her to a place with such a romantic atmosphere.

After they placed their drink orders, Phillip escorted Serenity to the antipasto and salad bars. Serenity opted for a Caesar salad, while Phillip selected an assortment of antipasti for himself. When they returned to their table, Phillip said, "You don't know what you're missing. These antipasti are the best."

"I'm good with this salad, thanks," Serenity replied.

"No wonder you're so thin. Don't you know that salads don't put any meat on the bones?"

"Oh, I'm going to eat more than this salad, trust me. I can't wait for my entrée."

By the time the server returned to take their orders, they'd had a chance to study the menu. Serenity ordered seared shrimp and scallops with an herb risotto, while Phillip ordered steak and smashed potatoes with a side of lobster tail. They made small talk until the food arrived. After a few bites of his steak, Phillip sighed contentedly. "I love this place. The food is always fantastic."

"I guess you bring a lot of women here, huh?" Serenity said.

"No; actually, I've come here with only one other woman."

Serenity raised an eyebrow.

"My ex-wife."

"Do you miss her?" Serenity asked, then immediately regretted prying when she saw the hurt look on his face.

"I used to. I thought we would be together forever, and it's taken me some time to realize that Chantel and I were never meant to be. Sometimes, the heart wants more than it can have."

"I don't think I will ever understand how two Christians can't make marriage work."

"Chantel and I got married before I gave my life to Christ. She never forgave me for that."

"For what? Getting saved and loving the Lord? Do you really expect me to believe that your ex-wife is that selfish?"

Phillip shook his head. "I won't disparage Chantel. Things just didn't work out between us, and I'd rather leave it at that. Okay?"

"Too touchy a subject for you?"

"I'll tell you what," Phillip said. He took a sip of water and then set the glass back down. "You show me your wounds, and I'll show you mine."

Did he really think that she was going to tell him about how Michael dumped her? That was not about to happen. "You can forget it. I don't bare my soul on first dates."

"So, is that what we're calling this? A date?"

"What would you call it, Phillip? Why would you bring me to a place like this if this isn't a date?" She waved a hand in the air as she glanced around the restaurant. "Everything about the atmosphere in this restaurant screams romance."

"Maybe I'm trying to tell you something."

She took a bite of shrimp and closed her eyes, savoring the taste. "You're going to have to speak up, because I don't read minds."

"Not even when you fast?" he asked jokingly.

Serenity pointed at the plate in front of her. "I just broke my fast. But, no, not even when I fast. So, spill it."

Phillip put his fork down and looked Serenity in the eye—a deep, penetrating gaze that made it feel like he was seeing into her soul. "I really wanted to come see you when I was in Chicago. But, at the same time, I was glad that I had to rush back home." He looked down at his plate for a moment, as if trying to get his thoughts together. When he raised his eyes to meet hers again, he said, "I don't know where this is going for us, but I haven't been able to stop thinking about you since we met in my office. But a good friend of mine told me to leave you alone until I got my head on straight."

"What's wrong with your head?" she asked, all the while praying inwardly that this fine man hadn't been hit so many times on the football field that he was suffering the latent effects of a concussion.

"I like you, Serenity, so I'm going to be straight with you. I've been feeling pretty down on myself lately because I'm a pastor, and I preach on forgiveness all the time, yet I haven't been able to forgive my ex-wife. But all that changed last week, once I finally realized that the divorce wasn't about me; it was about some need for security that Chantel didn't believe I could fill."

Oh, Lord, it's worse than a head injury. "Are you still in love with your ex-wife?" Serenity asked.

Phillip shook his head. "It's been two years since she left me, and a year since the divorce was final. Believe me, I've had more than enough time to get over any delusions of love."

The pain she saw in Phillip's eyes produced an almost physical sensation in her. This was no pride-filled preacher seated before her. He was just a man—a man who had loved and lost. His honesty spoke to her heart and allowed her to open up to him, as well. "You're not the only one with issues, you know."

"Are you trying to tell me that you're still in love with your ex-fiancé?"

"Oh, please. Far from it. Michael Randolph never really loved me. I was just a pretty little doll he wanted the world to know belonged to him. And then, when my popularity grew with my program, he started discouraging me, accusing me of trying to show him up. Instead of being supportive, he told me that I was too competitive and called off our wedding."

"Can you imagine how jealous he would have been if you were a noted pastor?" Phillip asked. "By the way, why did you decide not to become a pastor? You're a preacher, Serenity. It's in your blood."

"You've been honest with me, so I'm going to do the same with you." She hesitated for a moment, and then began, "As a preacher's kid, I've seen the good, the bad, and the ugly parts of ministry. And even though I've known since I was a child that God wanted me to minister the gospel to His people, I sought to find a way to do that and have as little close interaction with His people as possible, thereby decreasing opportunities for betrayal. My television ministry made that possible."

"Well, I can honestly say that I've never met a preacher who was afraid of people," Phillip said with a smile.

"I'm not afraid of them, just cautious. I've seen my father and brother hurt and disappointed by people they had trusted so many times that I just don't want to go through that."

"I hate to break it to you, Serenity, but betrayal is a part of life."

"That's why I don't like getting to know people on such a personal level. It hurts too much when things go wrong."

"You're forgetting one thing, Serenity. Jesus didn't have the luxury of deciding how He would serve God. He couldn't just go to God and say, 'It hurts too much when these people betray Me, so I don't want to have a going-to-the-cross kind of ministry.'"

Serenity leaned back in her seat, not willing to acknowledge that Phillip had hit a nerve. "I told you I have issues," she said, hoping that brief reiteration would end their discussion.

Phillip shook his head. "I never would have guessed. A prominent Christian talk show host who fears intimacy."

Serenity rolled her eyes and took another bite of shrimp.

"No, really. You have a problem with developing real and meaningful relationships, and I'd like to help you with that, if you'll let me."

She narrowed her eyes. "And how are you supposed to help me?"

"Come to church with me tomorrow and find out."

Ten

PHILLIP WAS LEAFING THROUGH HIS BIBLE AND RE-
viewing the Scriptures for that morning's message when Derek barged into his office. "You
brought her to church with you today?" he said, incredulous.

Phillip looked up. "I'm going over my sermon, Derek.
Can this wait?"

"Oh, no. You're not getting off the hook that easy. I
thought you said you weren't going to approach her until
you got everything straightened out with Chantel!"

Closing his Bible, Phillip said, "I had a discussion with
Chantel, and I think I'm moving forward."

"Did you tell Serenity about Chantel?"

"Not everything," Phillip admitted.

"Well, you'd better get to talking, because we both
know that your crazy ex-wife is not going to let you live
in peace—or any woman who gets involved with you."

"See, that's why you were always getting beat down
on the field," Phillip countered. "You've got no heart. No
faith."

"You've lost your mind, just like Chantel. I dominate
on that field, and you know it."

"That's what your mouth says, but I've got films that
say something different." Phillip stood up and grabbed
his Bible.

"Well then, get your camera out, because I'm calling this a game day. You're going to get punished, son."

"Get your best people and bring it," Phillip said as he walked out of his office and stepped into the pulpit area. When the praise team finished their last song, Derek stepped up to the podium and welcomed the congregation. He invited the visitors to stand up, and Phillip scanned the sprinkling of people standing in the front, middle, and back pews, as well as in the balcony. Each week, it seemed that the Lord was leading more and more people to New Destiny Church. Phillip was humbled by what God was doing. Other people had tried to talk him out of constructing a church with twice as much space as they needed at the time, but God had been whispering in his ear that he was going to need those extra seats. So, he'd ignored the naysayers and looked expectantly to the future.

Phillip noticed that Serenity hadn't stood up with the other visitors. She probably didn't want to be noticed; that way, she wouldn't have to reach out to anybody. But he was going to rectify that. When it was his turn to take the microphone and step behind the podium, he told his congregation, "We have a very special guest with us today, and I would be remiss if I didn't introduce her to my family."

Phillip looked down at Serenity, who had an expression of horror on her face, like she thought he was about to unleash a gang of unrepentant churchgoers on her. She had no idea. "Stand up, Ms. Serenity Williams. I want all of New Destiny Church to give you a warm welcome."

Serenity reluctantly stood up and waved.

"Isn't she beautiful?" Phillip said, even though he knew he shouldn't have said something so personal, but he had the can't-help-its again. He looked around the church. "Where are my greeters?" When several women stood up, he told them, "Come up here and give Ms. Williams a hug. Make her feel welcome in our house."

One by one, women from all over the sanctuary lined up to give Serenity a hug. Phillip noticed that she was a bit stiff at first, but, after about the tenth hug, she started to smile and return each embrace with more enthusiasm. Once the line of huggers diminished and the commotion quieted down, Phillip began his sermon. During the message, the congregation got fired up, and he noticed that even Serenity stood up and whooped with the rest of them a few times.

When the service was over, Phillip asked Serenity to stand at the sanctuary door and help him greet the parishioners as they left the church.

"This really isn't necessary, Phillip. I know what you're trying to do, but I'm not afraid to talk to people."

"Oh, yeah? Prove it," he said as he took her hand and guided her toward the sanctuary door.

She whispered in his ear, "Your congregation is going to get the wrong idea about us."

"If they think that you are very special to me, they'll be right."

Shaking her head, Serenity turned away from him and greeted an elderly woman who was exiting the sanctuary.

"I hope you're staying around for a while," the woman said. "I haven't seen Phillip smile this much in years."

"That's not true, Grandma," Phillip leaned over to say. "I couldn't stop grinning the night we celebrated your eighty-fifth birthday."

The woman gave him a playful poke in the arm. "What did I tell you about calling out my age as if it's your shoe size or something?"

"Sorry, Grandma. It won't happen again."

As his grandmother walked off, Phillip greeted a couple of other people and then leaned toward Serenity and said, "The next time you're in town, I'll introduce you to my mom."

"Who says I'm coming back to Tampa?" Serenity asked as she continued shaking hands and greeting the people who came through the doors.

When the sanctuary was empty, Phillip said, "Now, I've got a football game to win, and you, Ms. Serenity Williams, can be my cheerleader."

"No can do, Pastor McKnight. I have a plane to catch."

Looking wounded, Phillip said, "Your flight doesn't leave until five in the evening. Why would you want to sit all alone in an airport terminal when you could be in a park, meeting friends and cheering for me?"

She looked at her watch. "Okay, I'll go, but no pom-poms. I didn't make the cheerleading squad in high school, and I really don't want to relive that trauma."

"What? I can't believe you didn't make the cheerleading team. You look better than any cheerleader I've ever known."

"Two left feet," Serenity said with a shrug.

"I don't care if you have two left arms; you can cheer for me any day of the week."

"Phillip," Serenity chided him, "please stop saying things like that."

"Am I making you uncomfortable?"

"Just a tad," she admitted with a smile.

Phillip wanted Serenity to know that he was very serious about trying to get to know her. But the last thing he wanted was to make her uncomfortable. So, he said, "Okay. I'll behave."

Serenity and Phillip must have had two totally different ideas about what behaving looked like, because Serenity wouldn't have guessed that running a touchdown while screaming, "Look at me, Serenity!" or tackling a guy and then looking over at her and asking, "Where's my cheering section?" meant that Phillip was behaving himself.

Serenity was ten seconds away from complete mortification when a pretty woman in a pink jogging suit walked over to her and held out her hand. "Hi, I'm Derek's wife, Missy."

"Nice to meet you," Serenity said, shaking her hand. "Derek is one of the elders at New Destiny, right?"

"Yeah," Missy said, turning to point at her husband, who was strutting onto the field with the ball. "He's also the other lunatic quarterback out there." Missy shook her head and rolled her eyes. "Neither Phillip nor Derek got to be the quarterback during their professional careers, so now, when they play, they can't be on teams with each other because they both want to be quarterback."

"Boys," Serenity said, shaking her head empathetically.

"Boys, indeed," Missy agreed, then switched the subject. "Phillip sure seems happy to have you here. I hope you're going to stay for a while."

"I'm actually flying out today. I've got to get back home to Chicago."

"That's too bad."

"What is going on with everybody? You all act like the man spends his days moping around or something. But that's not what I have seen at all. Phillip is full of energy and life. He'll do just fine, whether I'm here or not."

"He has good days and bad days, but none has been as good as today seems to be. He looks happy again. I've missed that in Phillip."

Serenity watched Phillip run up and down the make-shift football field. He commanded the team like the two-time Super Bowl champion he would forever be re-membered as. But he also handled his business behind the pulpit. It hadn't escaped her notice how attentive the congregation was when he spoke. People leaned forward, took notes, talked back, and whooped and hollered. He was a man who impressed others easily, yet, somehow, Serenity saw so much that was humble within him, and so much that was unresolved. She just wasn't sure if she was the person to help him resolve his issues, especially when she had issues of her own to iron out. Now that she had openly admitted her distrust of church members, she felt cynical—and that bothered her.

As she continued to cheer for Phillip and his team, she noticed a woman in three-inch heels, denim cutoff shorts, and a shirt that exposed her belly button. Serenity was a Chicago girl accustomed to subzero temperatures in February, and therefore would never dream of coming out of the house in shorts in the wintertime. But this was Tampa, and the temperature was sixty-five today. *Live and let live*. The woman was probably an ex-cheerleader reliving her glory days of walking around football fields half-naked.

Moments later, the woman came over and held out a hand to Serenity. "Hello, I'm Chantel McKnight."

"Hi," Serenity said, taking her hand. "I'm Serenity Williams."

"Oh, I know who you are," Chantel said, her upper lip curling as if she had tasted something sour.

Missy cleared her throat. "Hey, Chantel! Girl, we didn't know you were coming out to the game today."

"I guess you wouldn't know, since I haven't heard from you since Phillip and I split up," Chantel said, letting her claws show.

"Well, I was getting ready to introduce Serenity to a few of our fellow church members. You don't mind, do you, Chantel?"

"I was talking to her, but I know you don't care," Chantel said, then turned, swinging her long, flowing hair, and stomped off in a huff.

"Thank you," Serenity whispered to Missy. "I don't know what that was all about, but that woman seems vicious."

"You don't know the half of it. I've been praying for Chantel ever since the day I met her. I still don't know what Phillip saw in that woman in the first place."

"Isn't it obvious?" Serenity asked with a chuckle.

Missy turned to watch Chantel strut her long legs to the other side of the field. She laughed. "Yeah, it's obvious."

Missy stood by Serenity's side until the game was over. The two women talked, laughed, and cheered for the two teams. Serenity liked Missy. She seemed friendly and fun, like Melinda—like someone she wouldn't mind being friends with.

Phillip approached with the grin of a winner. "See, I knew I needed you cheering for me."

"It might have been Chantel's cheers that helped you win," Serenity said, even though she knew she was being snarky without a cause. Phillip had barely even looked in Chantel's direction.

Not taking the bait, Phillip put an arm around Serenity's shoulders. "I need to get you to the airport," he said.

Serenity looked at her watch and saw that it was two thirty. "Oh, my goodness. Yes, we need to go." She turned to Missy and said, "It was so nice meeting you. Thank you for keeping me company."

"Not a problem. I hope to see you around Tampa again real soon," Missy told her.

Phillip drove like a madman in order to get Serenity to the airport by three. During the drive, she decided to bring up the subject of Chantel again, trying to be extra discreet. "So, does your ex-wife come to your games often?"

"Very rarely anymore, but I haven't invited her to a game since we split up. Chantel doesn't like football and was always irritated by the time the games ended."

Not wanting to pry any further, Serenity turned the conversation to the game itself. "You were a real MVP today. Do you miss playing professionally?"

"Sometimes, but what I have now is so much more important to me than football ever was. I was ready to go when I retired."

"You sound like a man who knows what he wants."

"And you sound like you're still interviewing me," he said, chuckling. "But, yes, I do know what I want."

When they arrived at Tampa International Airport, Phillip stopped at Serenity's terminal, got out of the car, and took her suitcase out of the trunk. He moved to the passenger door, set the suitcase on the ground, and opened Serenity's door to help her out, his eyes focused intensely on her. "I want to spend more time with you, Serenity Williams," he said as she got to her feet. Then, without warning, Phillip lowered his head and touched her lips with his own.

The kiss was timid, at first—two people getting to know each other. But as Serenity wrapped her arms around Phillip and closed her eyes, the kiss grew in passion and hunger. At that moment, she felt cherished, like a first rose given to a woman in love. But the thought of finding love with a man like Phillip—another preacher—terrified her. Serenity opened her eyes and stepped out of Phillip's embrace. She looked down at her watch and said, "I'd better get in there."

Phillip didn't move out of her way. "If you miss your flight, you'll be stuck here with me. I think I like that."

She wanted to tear up her ticket and say that she would stay in Tampa forever, but she had given her heart away once before to a man full of promises for tomorrow—promises that fell short. She would never let that happen to her again. "I can't stay, Phillip. I've got a lot of work waiting for me in Chicago."

He relented and stepped out of her way. "I'll let you go today, Serenity. But, who knows? Maybe, one day, you'll realize that you belong right here with me."

Eleven

SERENITY DIDN'T BELONG IN TAMPA WITH PHILLIP. SHE was meant to be in Chicago with her family and her ministry. So, why couldn't she stop thinking about him? It was that kiss—the fiery, passionate, never-want-it-to-end kiss they'd shared before she'd left Tampa. And now, everything had gotten all jumbled up and turned around in her head. But, if she was honest with herself, that had happened before the kiss. Phillip had captured her heart the day she'd met him—and every day after that. During their dinner at Armani's, Phillip had won her over again by just being himself. He'd opened up to her and revealed more of himself to her than she'd ever expected him to.

Phillip had left several messages for her this week on her home phone and at the studio, but Serenity couldn't deal with him right now. She needed to get her emotions in check before she had another conversation with him. In the midst of her musings, Pam walked into her office and sat down. She was holding a package, and, from the look on her face, Serenity could tell that she didn't like the contents. "What's that about?" she asked, nodding toward the package.

"It's another media kit from Michael."

She should have known. The week after the ratings had doubled due to Phillip's appearances, Michael had sent in his media kit and demanded an interview—a chance to show off his preaching skills. Serenity had ignored him and gone about her business. The next week, one of the executives from the Word network had contacted Pam and thrown out Michael Randolph's name as someone they should seriously consider interviewing. And now, Michael had the gall to send them his media kit again, as if they hadn't received the first one.

Serenity wanted to call Michael and explain exactly why she didn't want to interview him, but then she changed her mind. "Contact him and schedule the interview," she told Pam.

Pam's eyes just about popped out of her head. "Excuse me?"

"I'm serious, Pam. Let's do this interview with Michael. You never know—maybe our ratings will double again."

Pam stood up. She had a curious look on her face, but she said, "If that's what you want, I'll make it happen."

As Pam opened the door to leave, Serenity said, "Make it happen quickly, okay, Pam?"

Nodding, Pam closed the door behind her.

This was exactly what she needed. She had been caught in some type of vortex that allowed her to see the good in preachers again, and it was all because of how forthcoming and humble Phillip appeared to be. But spending a little time with Michael would remind Serenity why she had decided never to date another preacher. Yes, this would be perfect.

Serenity leaned back in her seat and exhaled, feeling at ease—that is, until she started sorting through her mail and opened a note that read, "You're not listening. Stay away from him."

She sat up straight in her chair, truly confused. She *was* staying away from Phillip; she hadn't returned any of his calls. So, why was someone still bugging her about him? Had Michael found out that she'd been in Tampa with him this past weekend? Michael was the one who had called off the wedding, so why should he care if she was seeing Phillip or not? She didn't know the answer to any of the questions swirling around in her head, but she intended to get to the bottom of them when Michael arrived at the studio for his interview.

On Wednesday of the following week, when Michael walked into the studio, Serenity wished she had given this interview another thought. He looked suave and in charge with his light-gray suit and baby-pink necktie. In his hand were a dozen red roses, and he was grinning like he had a hotline to heaven. Serenity didn't even like roses, but Michael had never bothered to figure that out.

"Hey, beautiful," Michael said as he handed her the bouquet.

Serenity took the roses and laid them on the table, then pointed to the room behind her. "The hair and makeup professionals are in there, waiting on you."

Michael stepped back so she could take in the full view of him. "I'm not like that pretty boy you had on the show a month ago. I don't need all that touch-up stuff."

It was just like Michael to try to put Phillip down. In reality, Phillip's rugged good looks tipped him over the fine-o-meter like no one else's Serenity had ever seen, but he wasn't a pretty boy. That was Michael, the Shemar Moore look-alike himself. "If you don't want to use our hair and makeup people, that's fine, Michael. You can have a seat in the green room, and Pam will let you know when we're ready for you."

She turned and started walking away when Michael said, "Wait, Serenity. You're forgetting your roses."

She swiveled, grabbed the bouquet, and continued to her office. Inside, she closed her door, stood in the middle of the room, and threw the roses in the air, letting them fall haphazardly around her. Michael had played her for a fool once, and she'd sworn she would have nothing else to do with him. Now, she had let him pressure her into interviewing him. She sat down in her chair and drummed her fingers on the desk, thinking about the situation she'd gotten herself into. The more she thought about it, the more she blamed Phillip for this turn of events. If he hadn't jumbled her brain with that kiss, she never would have been willing to put herself through spending an hour with the Reverend Michael Randolph.

There was a knock, and before Serenity could invite the person in, the door swung open. It was Michael. "I thought I'd sit in here with you, rather than wait in the green room by myself," he said as he stepped into the office. When he noticed the roses on the floor, he said, "You're still mad at me, huh?"

She didn't answer the question. "What can I do for you, Michael?"

"I've missed you, Serenity. I just wanted to talk to you for a few minutes." He gave her that half-cocked smile that always softened her up. "For old times' sake."

She smiled at Michael—it was the first smile she'd given him since they'd broken up. "Sit down, Michael," she said, propping her elbow on the desk and resting her chin in her hand. "You're right—we should catch up."

Michael unbuttoned his suit jacket and sat down. On the outside, he appeared so self-assured and in control. And he had every right to be, because Michael had it all.

He had been blessed with good looks and a passion for the Lord, and he was on his way toward greatness in the kingdom of God. What Serenity didn't understand was why his inward self didn't jibe with his outward act. Because Michael was one of the most insecure men she had ever known.

"The church has been growing. I've got almost a thousand members."

"I knew that would happen for you. Your ministry has purpose, so it's bound to grow," Serenity said. She wasn't just trying to flatter Michael, either. Although she found him egotistical, she believed that he loved the Lord and desired to do God's will. He just needed to stop trying to grab everyone's attention and let God make him what he was destined to be. But it wasn't her problem anymore, so all she could do was pray for Michael and keep moving on.

"Yeah, I know you've always believed in my vision." Then, in a wistful tone, Michael said, "I just wish things had turned out differently for us."

It was weird for her to realize, but she wasn't hoping that Michael's words meant that he had finally come to his senses, in her mother's words. God had intervened in their relationship, and Serenity was more than okay with the outcome. Yet, to be quite honest, Serenity found herself agreeing with Melinda that she wasn't willing to give male preachers a fair shot. Maybe seeing Michael today was helpful, after all—it reminded her about some of the good things she knew about him. Standing up, she said, "It is really nice seeing you today, Michael. Now, let's go tape your interview."

Michael stood up. "Before we begin, I have something else I need to tell you."

There was a nervous look on Michael's face, which made Serenity curious. "What's up?"

He lowered his eyes. "I met someone."

Serenity arched an eyebrow, as if to say, "And?"

"Her name is Karen, and I plan to ask her to marry me."

Serenity came around the desk with her arms open wide. "That's great, Michael." They hugged, and Serenity added, "I hope she makes you happy."

"She does, Serenity. She's not like we were. Karen is as far removed from the ministry as anyone I know. If you put a microphone in her face, she gets nervous. But I like that about her."

"You made the right decision, then. You should bring her around sometime," Serenity said without feeling an ounce of jealousy. But she did wonder if she would have acted this charitably toward Michael if Phillip hadn't kissed her. As they were heading toward the set to begin the interview, she remembered the threatening e-mail she had received. She stopped in her tracks. "Michael, I need to ask you something."

Michael stopped, turning to face her. "Yes?"

"Just after my interview with Phillip McKnight, did you send an e-mail, asking me to leave Phillip alone?"

A puzzled look crossed his face. "Why would I do that?"

"I don't know. Never mind."

What did this mean? If Michael hadn't sent her that e-mail, did that mean she had a stalker? Or had the e-mail been nothing more than a practical joke?

Serenity put on a composed smile and escorted Michael to the set.

◡◠

When Phillip turned on his television that evening to catch Serenity's show, he was dumbfounded to see that she was interviewing Michael Randolph, her ex-fiancé.

"Why would she have him on her program?" he wondered aloud. From what Serenity had told him, Phillip had
assumed that she didn't care much for her ex. But they
seemed pretty chummy right now. Serenity was practically giddy while interviewing the man.

Phillip knew that he shouldn't even be watching the
show. He had his Bible open and was trying to review
his sermon for tonight's Bible study. But he couldn't help
himself. As a matter of fact, Phillip was hoping Serenity
would open up the phone lines and invite viewers to call
in to the show. He would call and ask what in the world
she was doing with Michael. But, before his jealous de-
mon could rear any higher, someone knocked on his office door. He turned off the television and said, "Come in."

Chantel stormed into his office. "We need to talk," she
said.

Chantel knew that his church had Bible study on
Wednesday nights, and that he didn't like being disturbed
on the days he had to deliver sermons. But she had never
cared about the things that mattered to Phillip. "I'm busy
right now, Chantel. Can this wait?"

"I've called you three times since I saw you and that
woman at the football game. You haven't returned any of
my calls, so I figured you'd talk to me face-to-face."

"I've been really busy, Chantel. I haven't had time to
call you back yet."

"It looked like you had time for Serenity Williams.
What was that all about? Because I *know* she's not still taking notes for her show. Maybe she's taking notes for something else?" Chantel said, her voice dripping with venom.

When Phillip didn't respond, Chantel pulled a chair
around behind Phillip's desk so that she could sit next
to him. She grabbed his hands and held them in hers as

she said, "I've been thinking about all the things you said while we were going through the divorce, and I feel like such a fool now, because I should have listened to you."

"About what?"

"You said that we belonged together, and that, if we truly loved each other, we could work out our differences. But I wouldn't listen. I was so angry with you for spending all of our money on this church."

"That's not true." He pulled his hands away from Chantel. "I wasn't spending all of our money. But I sure didn't see the harm in putting whatever amount of money I wanted toward the building of God's kingdom."

Chantel lifted her hands. "It's over and done with now, Phillip. I didn't come here to rehash the past with you. I just miss you, baby. And I want you to come home."

Chantel had on a form-fitting blouse and a short skirt, so Phillip could see every curve and those long legs of hers. When he'd dated Chantel, he hadn't known Christ, and, therefore, hadn't known how to love, only how to lust. Her tricks had worked on him then. But the new man within him wasn't the least bit moved by all the womanly flesh before him. He needed something more—a woman who had a heart for ministry and understood how important serving God was to him. So, he opened his mouth and said words he wouldn't have dreamed of saying six months ago. "I'm sorry, Chantel, but I don't think we are right for each other."

She jumped out of her seat. "What do you mean, we're not right for each other? We were married, Phillip."

"And you left me, even after I begged you to stay. Chantel, I would have done anything to make our marriage work. But there was no convincing you of that. You were miserable with me, and I couldn't do anything about it."

"All you had to do was stop spending our money on this church, and I would have been happy."

"Everything I have is from God, Chantel. Why shouldn't I show Him that I appreciate all that He has given me by giving back to Him and His kingdom?"

"This has nothing to do with God, and you know it. You're sneaking around with that Serenity Williams, and you think I'm just going to stand by and let you go." She put her hands on her hips. "You should know me better than that, Phillip."

"I don't know you at all, Chantel. I thought I knew you. When we got married, I truly thought you loved me."

"I do love you, baby."

Phillip stood up and moved out from behind his desk. He was feeling confined and needed to put some space between him and Chantel. "I think you loved the *idea* of you and me. But you loved having money even more than you loved the idea of us."

Shaking her head, Chantel said, "It wasn't like that, Phillip. I grew up poor, and I wasn't going to let you put me back in the poorhouse. I know you, Phillip. You don't care about the money. For you, it's all about the mission you're on. But I'm not with all that. I just want to be with you."

"As long as I've got some money, you mean."

"I don't need you to have any money, Phillip. I have money now, and it's safe from all your foolish squandering."

Phillip looked at Chantel as if seeing her for the first time. Yes, he knew she was selfish, but this was too much for him.

⁂

Chantel wasn't about to let Phillip go simply because of a little thing like a divorce. He didn't understand her at all. She'd never wanted to leave him. She just didn't want him to give all their money to that church. Their marriage had been perfect before he had gone and fallen in love with Jesus. Before that day, all he'd thought about had been how he could make her happy. Did he think he could just dismiss her now because he'd found another woman?

As far as Chantel was concerned, she had invested five good years into her marriage with Phillip. Plenty of couples reconciled and remarried after divorcing. And, now that she had safeguarded her money and had no reason to worry that he would throw all of their cash in the air as a sacrifice to God, she wanted her man back. And she would do whatever it took to make that happen.

She picked up her cell phone and dialed a number. When someone picked up on the other end, she said, "I need your help."

"That's usually the only time you call me. What's up?"

"Meet me at my house, and I'll tell you exactly what I need you to do." When she hung up the phone, Chantel was smiling and counting the days until Phillip was back in her arms.

Twelve

SERENITY WAS JUST FINISHING UP A PROGRAM WHEN Phillip walked into the studio. She tried to remain professional and in tune with the flow of the Spirit as she prayed for her viewers and closed out the broadcast, but Phillip's presence dominated her thoughts. He looked so good as he walked toward her in a brown, leather bomber jacket and denim jeans, which accentuated his slightly bowlegged walk. Somehow, she made it through, and the camera finally stopped rolling. Her knees were shaking, and her heart was racing, but she was determined not to let him know how excited she was to see him. "Hey! I didn't know you were coming to Chicago this weekend," she greeted him.

"If you would have answered any of my calls, I would have told you," Phillip said, stuffing his hands in his pockets.

He seemed unsure of himself, and Serenity couldn't understand why. Anyone who kissed like he did should know where he stood. But she would be the last person to tell him. "I've been busy, Phillip. And I don't think you should show up here without calling first. You could have told me in one of your messages that you were coming to town." She turned away from him and started walking to her office.

Phillip followed her into her office and closed the door behind him. "So, you admit that you got my messages?"

Exasperated, Serenity threw up her hands and then let them fall at her sides. "Of course, I got your messages, Phillip. I just don't know what to say to you."

Phillip sounded just as exasperated as he said, "You can start by telling me what's going on with you and Michael."

"What are you talking about?" she quirked her brows, feeling completely confused.

"You interviewed him the other day. From what you told me, I didn't even think you were on speaking terms with the man."

"We're not. But Michael kept sending his media kit to the studio, demanding an interview, and I just wanted to get it over with."

"The *Walk This Way* program means too much to you, Serenity. You don't let just anybody on it. So, why him?"

"Just because I think Michael is an egomaniac doesn't mean he has nothing valuable to offer the Christian community." She sat down at her desk and took off her heels. "Stop being so jealous. The only thing Michael wanted from me was an interview."

"How can you know that for sure?"

She grabbed her boots from under her desk, pulled them on, and stood back up. "He's in love with someone else, okay? Her name is Karen, and he's getting ready to pop the question."

"Oh," was all Phillip said before a smile crept across his face.

"What's that smirk on your face all about?"

"Nothing. Look...I just want to take you to dinner."

Serenity put her hands on her hips. "You flew to Chicago just to take me to dinner?"

He shrugged. "I missed you."

Caught off guard by how good it felt to hear Phillip admit that he missed her, she relaxed her stance and stopped pretending. "I've been thinking about you all week, too."

Phillip sounded almost pitiful as he asked, "Then, why haven't you returned any of my calls?"

What could she say? She had desperately wanted to talk to Phillip this week, but they had issues that she didn't know how to fix. First of all, Phillip was a preacher, and she had sworn off all preachers, even though she could see that Phillip was not egotistical and she believed that he respected her ministry. But then, they had another problem—dealing with a long-distance relationship. She chose to point that out. "Look at what you just did. You wanted to see me, so you had to get on a plane to make that happen. I'm just not sure I can deal with a long-distance relationship."

"Would I rather that you lived in Tampa? Of course, I would. But the simple fact is, the woman I want to spent time with lives in Chicago—and I'm willing to travel the distance to see her."

Serenity walked over to him and raised a hand to touch his cheek. "Why'd you have to say something so sweet like that?"

Gently enclosing her hand in his own, Phillip said, "It's the way I feel. I tried to stay away from you, but I need you in my life, Serenity. I'm just praying that you need me just as much."

This time, when their lips met, there was no shock or surprise in the move, just the meeting of two people fully able to acknowledge the feelings that were growing between them. "So, what's next?" Serenity asked when they finally separated.

Phillip leaned his forehead against hers. "Now, we get to know each other better. I call—and you answer the phone."

Serenity giggled.

"I'll come to see you, and you'll come to see me."

"Like a couple?" she asked. For some reason, it was important to her to know exactly where she stood with Phillip. She didn't want to be the only one thinking she was in a relationship; she'd been there and done that with Michael. The wounds from that humiliation had barely healed, so she wasn't looking to get burned again.

"That's exactly what I want. Let's be a couple, Serenity."

Suddenly, she covered her mouth with her hand and stepped away from Phillip. When she spoke, her voice was filled with sadness. "I can't date you, Phillip."

He arched an eyebrow. "What do you mean? You just kissed me, and you admitted you've been thinking about me."

"You're now a part of my father's fellowship. Michael's church had been part of my father's fellowship before we broke up, and then Michael took his church out of the fellowship and severed all ties with my father." Walking in circles, she said, "I can't risk putting my father through that again."

Phillip pulled her into his arms and kissed her cheek. "Your father already knows how I feel about you. And he's fine with it."

Pushing him away, Serenity said, "You told my father about us?"

"And your mother."

"Phillip, you didn't," she said before he kissed her again.

"Let's get out of here and go get something to eat," he said, taking her by the hand.

"Did you drive here?" she asked as they walked out of the studio.

"Yes, I rented a car at the airport."

"Well, can you follow me home so I can drop off my car?"

"I would follow you anywhere, Serenity Williams." Phillip leaned down and placed a kiss on her forehead. She took her keys out of her purse and then walked over to her car. As she was unlocking the door, Phillip said, "You can't go anywhere in this car."

"Why not?"

"You have a flat." He walked around the car and said, "Strike that; you have two flat tires."

"How on earth could I have two flat tires?" Serenity asked as she joined Phillip on the passenger side of the car. "Well, I guess you're right." She pulled out her cell phone and called Triple A, explaining her predicament to the representative.

When she hung up, Phillip said, "Did you run over some glass or something on your way in to work this morning?"

"Not that I recall."

"Might have been a nail, but I don't see how you'd get a nail stuck in both tires."

She opened the passenger door and put her car key in the glove box. "I told Triple A that I would leave my key in the glove box, so, we can go to dinner now. They'll call me when the car is ready."

"Do you think that's safe?"

"Who is going to steal a car with two flat tires? I'm not worried. Let's go get something to eat. I'm starving."

They got in Phillip's rental car and drove to a nearby Mexican restaurant Serenity recommended on account of the exemplary service and the outstanding, authentic food. They were seated in a corner booth, where they studied the menu and munched on homemade tortilla chips and salsa. Phillip ordered chicken nachos, and Serenity went for a burrito with rice and beans.

Not long after they placed their orders, someone approached the table, and Serenity was surprised to think that their meals were coming already. But when she looked up, she saw Michael standing there, holding the hand of an attractive woman.

"Hey, Serenity. I see you still love Mexican food," Michael said.

She gave him a smile, wondering if Phillip had something to do with the fact that her anger with Michael seemed to be seriously diminishing. "Hey, Michael. How are you doing?"

"Things are going well. I've received requests for tons of speaking engagements in just the two days since our interview."

"I'm happy for you, Michael." She then looked at Phillip and said, "Phillip, I'd like to introduce you to Michael Randolph." She looked back at Michael and said, "This is Phillip McKnight."

The two men shook hands, and then Michael put a hand on the back of the woman standing next to him. "This is Karen Larson."

Serenity smiled again as she extended her hand. "Hi, Karen. It's nice to meet you. Michael told me about you the other day."

Karen shook Serenity's hand and said, "Likewise. Michael has told me so much about you, I feel as if I already know you." Karen then turned to Phillip and said, "I saw you on Serenity's show a while back. I donated to your building fund."

"Thanks—I really appreciate it! We were able to get a lot accomplished with the money we raised from that program." Phillip reached across the table and took Serenity's hand. "Serenity has been a blessing to me since the moment I met her."

Michael put his arm around Karen and said, "I know what you mean. I feel the same way about Karen. Well, we'll see you around. I've got to get some food in my stomach."

"All right, Michael," Serenity said. "Thanks for stopping by. Oh—and, Karen? I'm glad I got the chance to meet you."

Once they were gone, Phillip leaned closer to Serenity. "I thought you said that Michael was engaged to Karen."

"He told me that he was going to ask her to marry him. Maybe he just hasn't done it yet."

"I've got to hand it to you, Serenity. Most women would be upset at seeing their exes with their new loves. Oh, they try to play it off and act like it doesn't bother them, but the eyes don't lie. When I look into your eyes, though, I don't see any sign that you're jealous of Michael."

"That's because I'm not. Michael is a part of my yesterday. I'm ready to see what tomorrow brings."

Just then, the server arrived with their food. Phillip said a prayer before they dug in. After a moment, he pointed at Serenity's plate. "How's your burrito?"

"Yummy. What about your nachos?"

"Great. I'm glad you picked this place, even if you've been here with Michael before."

"There's that green-eyed monster again."

Phillip lifted his hands in surrender. "Okay, you're right. I dined at the restaurant in Tampa with Chantel, but that wasn't the reason I took you there. I like the place. And you like this place, so it's all good."

"I like your attitude," Serenity said, then dug around in her purse for her phone, which was ringing. The caller

ID indicated that it was Triple A, so she answered it. And she couldn't believe the news.

"What's wrong?" Phillip asked as she snapped her cell phone shut.

"My tires were slashed."

"Why would anyone want to slash your tires?"

Setting her cell phone down on the table, Serenity said, "There's something I need to tell you." She lowered her head, trying to determine the best way to put this so that she didn't look silly for ignoring the warning signs.

"I'm listening," Phillip said.

"The last day of your segment, I received a threatening e-mail, telling me to stay away from you."

"Wait, wait," Phillip said, waving his hands in the air. "The e-mail referred to me, specifically?"

"No, but it said, 'Stay away from him. Don't make me tell you again'—or something like that. Then, a couple days after I came home from Tampa, I received a note with my regular mail. All this one said was, 'You're not listening.' Now, you show up in town, and my tires get slashed. This has to be about you, Phillip."

Phillip looked like he wanted to call a time-out or just flat-out start this game over. "There has to be some other explanation. Why would anyone terrorize you because of me?"

"Maybe you've got some crazy girlfriend you haven't told me about," Serenity said.

"You're the only woman I'm interested in, Serenity, and you're the only person I've dated since my divorce."

"Then it must be your ex-wife."

Phillip shook his head. "Chantel is a lot of things, but she's not a stalker or a tire slasher."

"Well, then, who could it be, Phillip? Because I'm not just imagining these things."

"Have you reported this stuff to the police?"

Serenity shook her head. "I received the first e-mail after Michael called me, complaining about having you as a guest on my show. So, I assumed he had sent the e-mail to scare me. But, after he told me about his upcoming engagement, I asked him if he'd sent the e-mail. He didn't know anything about it."

"Maybe he's just pretending. Maybe his whole 'I've got a girlfriend' claim is just an act to throw you off."

"I don't think so, Phillip. I really believe him. Michael didn't do it. So, maybe you need to go have a chat with Chantel."

"What am I supposed to say to Chantel?"

"Tell her that we're through, so she doesn't need to bother me anymore."

Phillip laughed.

"I'm serious, Phillip. I'm not interested in this type of drama. If your ex-wife is crazy, then I don't want to get involved with you."

Thirteen

That's absurd, Serenity. You can't just dismiss me over something we don't even know for sure is my fault," Phillip said, trying to get her to see reason. He'd just convinced this woman to give him a chance—no way was he going to throw in the towel because of some stalker!

Serenity ran her hand through her hair. "But, Phillip, what if it is Chantel? She gave me a strange look when I met her at your football game."

"Going from giving someone a strange look to slashing her tires is a far stretch, even for Chantel." Phillip held up a hand. "Look, let's just finish our dinner, then go to the police station and report this. Okay?"

Serenity nodded and took another bite of her burrito. But Phillip could tell that she was worried. He only prayed that their involvement had nothing to do with the threatening notes or her tires being slashed. He wouldn't be able to forgive himself if any harm came to her because of him.

When they arrived at the police station, Serenity and Phillip were told to wait in a small room with white walls, a long table, and two chairs. They sat down, and Phillip put his hand over hers. "We're doing the right thing," he assured her. "The police will catch whoever is behind this."

The door opened, and a brown-skinned man with a baby face walked in, carrying a folding chair. He sat down at the table across from them and extended his hand. "I'm Detective Roundtree."

Phillip and Serenity shook hands with the detective as they introduced themselves. Then, Roundtree asked, "How can I help you?"

"I'm here because someone has sent me a couple of threatening notes, and, tonight, the tires on my car were slashed," Serenity said.

Roundtree held out his hand. "Can I see the notes?"

"I don't have them with me, but one was sent to my e-mail account, and the other was just an anonymous note that had been left at my job with the regular mail."

"Where is the car?"

"It was parked at the studio where I work, but Triple A picked it up and changed the tires for me."

"That means we probably won't find much evidence there. But we can dust the envelope for prints," Roundtree said.

Shaking her head, Serenity said, "I threw it away. I also permanently deleted the e-mail."

Phillip couldn't believe that she would be so nonchalant about something like this. He turned to her and said, "How could you throw away potential evidence?"

"I told you, I thought it was Michael."

"Who is Michael?" Roundtree asked.

"Her ex-fiancé," Phillip said with a hint of contempt.

Serenity held up a hand. "I thought Michael might have sent the e-mail because he was jealous of Phillip or something. But Michael is a pastor. I highly doubt he would go around slashing tires."

"To be quite honest with you, ma'am, the anonymous e-mails and tire slashing fit the profile of a woman rather than a man."

Serenity jumped in her seat. "That's exactly what I told Phillip. I think his ex-wife is doing this stuff."

"Why is that?" Roundtree asked.

"Because none of this happened until after I interviewed Phillip on my television program."

Roundtree turned to Phillip. "Can you give me your ex-wife's name and address?"

"Sure, but she lives in Tampa, and I really don't think she's involved."

"Just give me her information, and I'll have the Tampa police talk to her," Roundtree said. He wrote down the information as Phillip gave it, then he turned back to Serenity and said, "I can't promise much, with so little to go on, but I can at least have the Tampa police speak with Mrs. McKnight to see if she's made any recent visits to Chicago."

"Thank you," Serenity said, standing up.

"Not a problem. My wife enjoys your program, so I don't want anything to happen to you," Roundtree said with a grin.

Phillip walked Serenity to his car and opened the door for her to get in. After he climbed in, he headed toward the Williams' house.

"Why did you bring me here?" Serenity asked as he pulled into her parents' driveway.

"I don't want you staying by yourself."

"What?" she scowled at him. "Maybe you haven't noticed, but I'm a grown woman. I don't need to run to my daddy for every little thing."

"I wish I had a daddy to run to. So, don't be so ungrateful that you have options others don't."

"What happened to your father?" she asked, her voice softer, gentler.

"He died when I was seventeen months old. Heart attack."

"I'm so sorry. How old was he?"

"He was only thirty-seven. I never told anybody, but that's why I retired two years ago—when I turned thirty-seven. I figured that if I was going to go out early, like he did, I wanted to go running touchdowns for the Lord rather than some rich team owner."

Serenity nudged Phillip's shoulder playfully. "All you have to do is eat right and exercise if you want to beat heart disease."

"Well, I guess I need to stay out of Italian and Mexican restaurants with you, then, huh?" He pointed toward her parents' house and asked, "Are we going in there?"

Rolling her eyes, Serenity opened the passenger door. "I'm not going because you want me to. I just really want to see my parents."

Phillip opened his door and got out of the car. "Whatever works for you, Serenity. But you need to tell your parents what's going on."

She turned around and stuck her tongue out at him.

"And you call yourself a grown woman!" he scoffed.

✑

"Mom, it's not like someone tried to kill me, so, please, calm down," Serenity pleaded with her mother, who was wearing out the rug in the family room.

"Serenity is right, Evelyn. Please stop pacing. You're making me nervous," Serenity's father told his wife. "Let's just sit down and figure out what we need to do in order to keep Serenity safe."

"You're right, Lawrence," her mother said, then sat down and asked everyone else to do the same. Her father sat down next to her on the sofa, and Phillip and Serenity lowered themselves into the love seat. "Okay, now, all I want is for my daughter to be safe, so please tell me how we're supposed to do that when we don't even know who's doing these things?" her mother asked.

"It's simple, Mom. Whoever this woman is, she's angry about Phillip, so, if I detach myself from him and keep my distance, the problem will be solved."

Phillip put his hand over Serenity's. "Serenity thinks that someone is angry because we're a couple."

"We're not a couple," she said, snatching her hand away. "There is too much drama around you, Phillip. I have enough to worry about by myself, and I'm not going to add you and your women to the list." Her anger was mounting, and, to avoid exploding, she stood up and stormed out of the room.

In the kitchen, she grabbed a green apple from the fridge, washed it off, picked up a knife, and started peeling the apple at a frenzied pace. Her mother walked into the kitchen and stood slightly behind her. "Are you okay, honey?"

"I'm fine, Mom. I just needed a break from the discussion."

"Do you think you might have been just a little too harsh with Phillip?" she asked with concern in her voice.

Serenity pulled out a chopping board and started slicing the apple. "Mom, I'm not used to this type of drama in my life. I keep to myself; I don't bother people, and they don't bother me. But, ever since I met Phillip, it's been constant drama."

"I'm just going to tell you what I see and let you make your own decision," her mother began. "I think Phillip really cares about you. And I just want you to take time to think about how you feel about him before making any snap decisions."

"Mom, someone slit my tires. Doesn't that scream, 'Run in the other direction'? Phillip needs to settle some things in his life before disrupting mine."

A look of sadness crossed her mother's face, but she quickly replaced it with a smile. "I'm on your side, Serenity, so you do what you need to."

"Thanks, Mom." Serenity arranged the apple slices on a plate and walked back into the family room. Phillip and her father were standing at the far end of the room, talking in low voices. When she cleared her throat, they turned to face her. "I'm going to spend the night at my parents', so I won't need you to drive me home, Phillip. And it's probably best that you leave, anyway, because I don't think we should see each other for a while."

"What's a while?" Phillip asked.

"I don't know. I'm not sure if we should see each other at all." Serenity saw the pain that danced through Phillip's eyes, but she was powerless to do anything about it. Even with a bishop for a father and a preacher, a politician, and a football player for brothers, she had managed to carve out a stable, peaceful existence for herself, and she liked it that way. Getting involved with Phillip would just complicate her life far beyond the limits of what she could handle.

"I understand if you need time to sort all of this out, but can I at least call or e-mail you from time to time?" Phillip asked.

She'd just told the man to take a hike, but he was standing in front of her parents, practically begging to be allowed to e-mail her. She had once begged Michael to reconsider his decision to cancel their wedding, but he had trampled on her heart, anyway. She wouldn't do that to Phillip. She offered him a small smile and said, "I would love for us to be friends, so please e-mail me anytime."

Fourteen

BACK IN TAMPA, PHILLIP TURNED HIS ATTENTION TO finishing the church building project and planning the celebration—anything to get his mind off of Serenity. He had put himself out there, put his heart on the line, and, for all his effort, she had told him that she only wanted to be friends. He didn't know if he could do that—not with the way he felt about her. But it was clear to Phillip that he wasn't going to do anything to change Serenity's mind in the near future, so he decided not to push.

"Why the long face?" Derek asked as he walked into Phillip's office.

"What?" Phillip looked up. "I must have been in a daze. Did you say something?"

"Yeah, I did. You've been in that same daze since you got back from Chicago."

"What's this?" Phillip asked as he pointed to the folder in Derek's hand, hoping to change the subject.

"The final bill from the contractor. They want it paid before their last day on the job."

Phillip could understand that. The real-estate market in Florida was dismal, and contractors were losing money left and right. He knew why they wanted the final payment before the job was finished, and he was more than willing to give it to them. He took the file from Derek and opened it. The amount was several thousand dollars lower than he had thought the payment would be. "That's a pretty good price," he said, surprised by the lack of emotion in his voice.

"He gave us a 10 percent discount," Derek said.

There was still no excitement in Phillip's voice as he said, "That was nice."

Derek rolled his eyes heavenward. "Man, why don't you just admit that you've got it bad for this girl and go for it?"

Phillip hung his head. "It's complicated."

Derek picked up the phone and handed it to Phillip. "Man, just call that woman and let her know how you feel."

He took the phone from him and hung it up. "I don't want to call her right now. But Missy did ask me to give Serenity a message, so I'll send her an e-mail, okay?"

With a smirk on his face, Derek turned to leave.

"What?" Phillip asked when he noticed that his friend seemed to be trying hard not to laugh in his face.

"Nothing," Derek said, opening the door. He then turned around to face Phillip. "You do realize that I'm going to tell the guys about this, don't you?"

"Whatever," Phillip said, then signed on to his e-mail account. Since he'd come back from Chicago, he'd been more diligent about reading his e-mails and listening to his phone messages, hoping that Serenity would check in. But she hadn't written or called, and he was beginning to think the whole matter was a lost cause. She wanted a drama-free life, and she held him responsible for the recent turmoil that had come her way. Therefore, she was willing to sacrifice him in order to get her life back in order. But no one could go through life without drama, pain, or hurt. That just wasn't the way it worked.

You play the hand you're dealt, taking the good with the bad, Phillip said to himself, as if composing a sermon. *You don't just give up and throw in the towel. You don't tell a man who wants a relationship with you that you just want to be friends when it's obvious you want the same thing he does. Well, okay—if it's friendship she wants, then she'll get it.*

He clicked on the new message icon and began typing an e-mail to Serenity.

Hey, Serenity. I just wanted to check on you. I haven't heard from you since I left Chicago on Saturday, and I was wondering how things were going. Also, Missy wanted me to say hello for her. She said that she really enjoyed hanging out with you at our football game when you were in town. Well, I guess I'd better sign off now. I have a sermon to write.

Phillip

Phillip closed his e-mail account and put his Bible in front of him. Before picking a Scripture on which to base his sermon, he bowed his head and prayed for guidance. He opened the Bible and turned to the book of Matthew and, before long, found himself in chapter fourteen, reading about Jesus walking on water in verses 26 through 31. He knew that this was where God wanted him.

When the disciples saw Him walking on the sea, they were troubled, saying, "It is a ghost!" And they cried out for fear. But immediately Jesus spoke to them, saying, "Be of good cheer! It is I; do not be afraid." And Peter answered Him and said, "Lord, if it is You, command me to come to You on the water." So He said, "Come." And when Peter had come down out of the boat, he walked

*on the water to go to Jesus. But when he saw that
the wind was boisterous, he was afraid; and beginning to sink he cried out, saying, "Lord, save
me!" And immediately Jesus stretched out His
hand and caught him, and said to him, "O you
of little faith, why did you doubt?"*

That was exactly what Phillip planned to talk to his
congregation about—having faith in Jesus, and relying on
that faith to have faith in other people rather than fearing or doubting them. He knew that he was just bringing
the issues in his personal life to his congregation, but he
couldn't help it. He was bothered by the fact that Serenity
didn't trust him to keep her safe.

He heard the familiar ding from his computer, indicating that he'd just received a new e-mail message. When
he looked at his computer and saw that the e-mail was
from Serenity, he quickly opened it.

Hey, Phillip.

I was starting to think that you weren't ever going
to e-mail me again. I hope that you're not too upset with me. I know that we've known each other
for only three months or so, but I have come to value your friendship, so please don't be a stranger.

I'm interviewing Smokie Norful today, so tune in
if you want to hear some good gospel music. I'll
also be wearing that baby-blue blouse I bought
with your money. ☺ Talk to you soon.

Serenity

Phillip looked at his watch. Serenity's show would be
on in another hour. So, he worked on his sermon a little

longer, then set it aside just in time to catch *Walk This Way*. Smokie Norful was one of Phillip's favorite singers, but Phillip barely even noticed that the man was on the show. He was too busy noticing how beautiful Serenity looked in baby blue. Then again, he thought she looked good in everything she wore.

When the show was over, he sent Serenity another e-mail. It simply said, "I loved the blouse...wish I could buy you a hundred more just like it." He then turned off the computer and left his office to check on the builders' progress. The building was supposed to be finished in two weeks, and then the whole church would celebrate with a mortgage-burning party.

Phillip found Jimmy Dayton in the fitness room, talking with Derek. Since the fitness room was really a playroom for him, Derek, and the other elders, it was the last room they'd asked Jimmy to work on, figuring that, if they ran out of money for some reason, the room could be finished in a rudimentary way. But God had made a way for them, and now the contractors were laying the drywall. "It's looking good in here, fellas," Phillip said as he approached the group.

Jimmy reached over to shake hands with Phillip. "My men will have the room finished in no time. Then, all that's left is some cleanup work."

"Thanks, man," Phillip said. "I'm just glad we could get this room done. I was worried that I shouldn't have cancelled my gym membership."

"Forget that. If I had to get in here and put up the drywall myself, this room was getting done," Derek said.

Phillip gave him a high five, and then his phone rang. Seeing that it was Chantel, he contemplated not answering. But, then, he realized that Chantel would just keep calling until he picked up, so he did. "What's up, Chantel?"

"Baby, I need you," she whined. "I really need your help."

He turned away from Derek and Jimmy and said, "We've been through this, Chantel. It's over."

"I fell down the basement stairs, Phillip, and I'm in pain. Please, come help me."

He looked heavenward, wishing that God would open the sky and give him a clue. Yet nothing came. So, he said, "I'll be right there."

"What's going on?" Derek asked as Phillip closed his phone and put it back in his pocket.

"Chantel hurt herself. I need to go check on her."

"No, you don't," Derek said.

Phillip put up his hands as he backed away from his friend. "Just leave it alone, okay?" As he left the church and drove to the house that used to be his, he realized that he wanted to help Chantel—but his desire to help had nothing to do with being in love with her. He wanted to help her, just as he would want to help any of God's children. He smiled, because he knew that God was granting his prayer; he was in the process of forgiving Chantel. He just hoped that she wasn't the one harassing Serenity, because that would make it a lot harder to forgive her.

When he arrived at the house, he jumped out of the car and ran up to the front door, then remembered that Chantel would have to let him in; she never kept the door unlocked unless she was expecting him. He pulled out his cell phone and called her. When she answered, he said, "Do you keep a spare key anywhere outside?"

"No—the door's unlocked."

"Oh. Gotcha," Phillip said as he tried the doorknob. Sure enough, it was unlocked, and as he walked inside, he wondered why. Chantel couldn't have come upstairs to unlock the door if she'd really been injured. Maybe she had been expecting someone else.

Phillip reached the door to the basement, opened it, and raced down the stairs two at a time. Chantel was in a heap at the bottom. He bent down and asked, "Tell me where it hurts."

She pointed, took a deep breath, and said, "My ankle."

He picked her up as if she were no bigger than a football and carried her up the stairs. Once they were in the car on their way to the hospital, he asked her, "Why didn't you call for an ambulance?"

"The 9-1-1 operators act funny when you don't call from a landline," Chantel explained.

He drove her to the emergency room and sat with her for hours while they waited to be seen. Once her ankle had been bandaged and she'd received her release papers, Phillip drove her home again. "Do you need anything?" he asked once he'd placed her comfortably on her bed.

"I need you to come back home."

Without hesitation, he said, "That's not going to happen."

Chantel pressed her lips into a pout. "But I can't do anything for myself. I need your help."

"I'll be right back," Phillip said, then turned and walked out of her room.

"What do you mean, you'll be right back?" she screeched. "You can't leave me by myself!"

Phillip wasn't listening. He knew that Chantel wouldn't be alone for long. She had a part-time cook and a maid who could put in some extra hours if she needed help. But he did have something that would help Chantel. So, he drove all the way home and found his crutches in the garage. They were adjustable, so, even though Chantel was shorter than he, she would have no problem using them.

He got back in his car and raced back to Chantel's house. When he came into her bedroom with the crutches, she looked insulted.

"What am I supposed to do with those?"

"These will help you get around, Chantel."

Rolling her eyes, she said, "If you stay with me, I won't have to get up. You can help me."

"I have a church to run; I can't stay here and be your personal servant. You have people you pay to do that, so I suggest you pick up that phone of yours and call one of them."

"Are you sure there isn't another reason why you can't stay?"

"I don't know what you're talking about, Chantel."

"That TV woman you brought down here a month ago—she's the reason you don't want to help me." She spat the words out as if her body would be contaminated if she didn't release them quickly.

"Serenity has nothing to do with this. You divorced me, remember?"

Chantel began screaming at him.

He laid the crutches against her bed and was walking out of the room when a thought hit him. Turning around, he said, "Were you expecting company today?"

Chantel stopped screaming. "No, why?"

"Your door was unlocked, and you normally do that when you know I'm coming. But how could you have known I was coming over here before you hurt your ankle?"

She rolled her eyes. "I didn't."

He walked out of the room without saying another word to her. He knew the truth, whether Chantel was willing to admit it or not. But the truth scared him. Because, if Chantel was willing to harm herself to get some attention from him, what was she willing to do to the person to whom he was giving his attention instead?

Fifteen

SERENITY HAD GOTTEN READY FOR WORK AND WAS checking her e-mail when her cell phone rang. She looked at the caller ID, saw that it was Melinda, and answered it. "Hey, girl! How are you and my soon-to-be godchild doing?"

"We're both doing well, but I want to know why you didn't tell me about your tires getting slashed."

"Who told you about tha—," Serenity began, then said, "wait—I already know. It was my bigheaded brother, who spoke at your revival last night, wasn't it?"

"Thank God he did, or I would still be in the dark."

"I just didn't want to worry you. And I don't think there's anything to worry about, anyway."

"Breaking it off with Phillip won't guarantee that this person will leave you alone—not if she's fixated on you."

"I guess Larry doesn't know everything. I didn't break it off with Phillip because there was nothing to break off. We were friends, and we still are. As a matter of fact, I was just reading an e-mail from him when you called."

"Oh, yeah? What's he talking about?"

Serenity smiled so broadly, she wouldn't have been surprised if Melinda could hear it through the phone. "The building project at New Destiny is complete, and the church is going to burn the mortgage next Sunday."

"Do you hear how you sound, Serenity? You're practically giddy over Phillip's good news."

"I'm happy for him. What's wrong with that?"

"If I didn't know better, I'd think you were burning the mortgage on your own church. Maybe that's it! Do you want to pastor Phillip's church with him?"

"The last thing I want to do is pastor a church, and you already know that."

"Yeah, but, Serenity, what if Phillip is the one? What if God's plan for you includes him and his church?"

"I hope God doesn't have that in mind for me. You know how I am, Melinda—I don't like it when people turn on each other, and they always turn on their pastors."

"Not all parishioners turn on their pastors, Serenity. Steven and I have a strong, close-knit congregation, and the people are loving and really care about the work of the ministry."

"You say that now, but those same people didn't lift a finger to help you when your father passed you over for the pastoral position."

"I love you, Serenity, but you need to stop being bitter."

"I'm not bitter. I just don't like putting myself in situations where people are likely to wrong me."

"You know you sound like a mental patient, right?"

"No, I don't, but we'll have to finish this conversation another time. I have to get to work." She and Melinda had been going round and round about this same subject for years. The two of them would never agree. Also the daughter of a bishop, Melinda had grown up in a similar environment. She'd watched her father try to make habitually unhappy people happy; she'd seen members who thought they knew more than the bishop and did whatever they wanted, no matter what prayerful advice they received. Melinda had seen the same things Serenity had, but she had chosen to believe that being a pastor brought more joy than pain. Serenity just wasn't there yet. "I'll talk to you tomorrow," Serenity said before clos-ing her phone.

Serenity was confused. She enjoyed communicating back and forth with Phillip online, but she was having trouble figuring out if she wanted the relationship to go any further. This was partly because Phillip's ex-wife was a loon, and partly because, if anything came of their re-lationship, Phillip would probably want her to pastor his church with him. She understood the logic behind it; you didn't sit a personality like Serenity Williams, a televi-sion show host with over a million viewers, in the front pew with a big, first-lady hat on her head. The natural thing would be for Serenity to work hand in hand with her preacher husband. Phillip had even admitted that he would expect his wife to work with him in the ministry. But Serenity wasn't cut out for hands-on ministry. It just wasn't her thing.

When it was her time to meet Jesus, Serenity wanted to be able to tell the Lord that she had planted and wa-tered good seed into the hearts and minds of the people who watched her program. It was her hope and prayer that each of her viewers would seek out a home church, where he or she could be spiritually fed and grow into ev-erything God intended. She liked evangelizing from afar because she didn't want to be held accountable for the lack of progress specific parishioners had in their walks with the Lord. Her attitude wasn't right; she knew that. But she had also grown up watching her father try to be a good witness and preach the gospel to people who refused to live right, no matter what he said and did to convict or encourage them.

Pastoring a church just wasn't the mission Serenity was made for. Sure, many people did it, and many of them even experienced success. She had heard the countless stories of church members growing in their faith and going on to do great things for the Lord. Preachers loved to talk about all the good their members were doing, like feeding the hungry, visiting the sick, and clothing the needy. She had heard stories of parishioners who had grabbed hold of the vision and founded battered women's shelters, food pantries, and other outreaches in their communities. All of that was great, but it seemed to Serenity that, for every positive story, there were ten stories of spiritually stagnant, do-nothing church members who practiced their faith solely during the Sunday service.

She wanted to know if the one member who grabbed hold of the vision was worth the ten who would never get it. She needed to go to God in prayer. So, she got down on her knees and began calling out to the Lord. "Father, I truly need You to help me see things the way You see them. Does my ministry bring a smile to Your face, or do You see it as a cop-out? Am I like the wicked servant who brought back no more than the same coin that his master had given him, or have I increased it five- or tenfold in Your eyes?"

Her heart was still heavy, so she continued to pray. She wanted nothing more than to please God and to serve Him wholeheartedly. Lately, though, she was beginning to wonder if she was in this with only half of her heart.

When Serenity finished praying, she got up, grabbed her keys, and left the house. Although she tried not to think about Phillip, thoughts of him kept dancing through her mind as she drove down the street. While she was stopped at a red light, she picked up her BlackBerry and checked her e-mail. She hated checking her e-mails in the car—she thought it an irresponsible practice—but technology had made it possible, and, since he was on her mind, she needed to know if she was on his.

Looking at her screen, Serenity figured that she wasn't on Phillip's mind, because he hadn't yet responded to the message she'd sent him that morning. She knew that she *was* on her stalker's mind, however, when she read the chilling subject line of a new e-mail: "You're going to pay for stealing his heart." The first threatening e-mail she had received had come from a generic, anonymous e-mail address, just letters and numbers. But this e-mail was from an address that began with CMcKnight1.

A car horn honked behind Serenity, and she realized that the light had turned green. She took her foot off the brake pedal and drove straight to the police station. "I've got you now, Chantel McKnight."

When she stepped inside the police station, Serenity approached the desk sergeant and asked to speak with Detective Roundtree.

"One moment; let me see if he's in," the woman said.

"Thank you," Serenity said, then took a seat in the waiting area.

In less than five minutes, Detective Roundree greeted Serenity in the waiting room. "Good morning, Ms. Williams. What brings you down here today?"

"I have evidence," she said, standing up and opening her e-mail file on her BlackBerry. "Now she's sending me these messages directly from her own e-mail address."

"Who is?" Roundtree asked.

Pointing at the screen, Serenity said, "That's Chantel McKnight's e-mail address. I'm sure of it."

Roundtree read the message, then looked back at Serenity. "E-mail that message to me. I'm going to see what's taking the Tampa police so long to get in touch with this woman."

"Thank you. I appreciate it," she said. After learning the detective's e-mail address, she sent the e-mail to him, then left the police station. It was after eight, and she needed to get to the studio to unlock the building for the crew. Pam had a key to the building, as well, but Serenity was usually the first to arrive every morning.

When she pulled up in front of the studio, she noticed that the door was wide open. Even if Pam had gotten there first, she wouldn't have left the door open like that. Serenity jumped out of the car and ran toward the building. When she stepped inside, her head began swirling. She felt nauseated at the sight before her. Her studio had been completely destroyed. It was as if Hurricane Katrina had hit Chicago. She stood in shocked silence until Pam arrived.

"God, have mercy," Pam said as she walked into the studio.

Serenity turned to face her with tears in her eyes. "What—? Why—? How could something like this happen?"

"I have no idea, but I'm calling the police," Pam said as she opened her cell phone and started dialing.

Serenity walked further into the rubble, wondering if her eyes were playing tricks on her. What kind of person would do something like this? Graffiti was all over the walls. But the graffiti didn't really bother her. With a little paint, they could take care of that in no time. What bothered her most was that the drywall had been pulled down from the structure on two of the walls, all of their furniture had been tossed around and ripped apart, and most of the equipment was missing.

She sat down on a chair with two broken legs and called her mother. By the time she picked up, Serenity's tears were flowing freely. "M-Mom, s-someone des—des—destroy—"

"Calm down, Serenity. Please tell me what's going on."

"Someone destroyed my studio," Serenity managed before letting out a loud sob.

"I'm on my way, Serenity. Just sit tight."

When she set down her phone, Pam came over to her, and the two women hugged. They both had poured their hearts and souls into this ministry, and, even though Serenity had recently wondered if she was doing the will of God halfheartedly, it felt like her whole heart was broken rather than just half of it.

"What are we going to do?" Pam asked.

"I don't know. I—I just don't know." Serenity had used all of her savings to construct the studio, and it had taken years and years to earn that money. She felt helpless and despondent.

Soon, the crew members started arriving, their jaws dropping in silent shock when they saw the damage. When everyone had gathered, the chatter began. Pam decided to show reruns until they could find another location or refurbish the studio. Fortunately, they had backup masters at a storage facility. One of the crew members ordered a couple of dumpsters so they could start throwing away the trash and putting things in order, but they found out that the dumpsters would not arrive until the next day.

When Serenity's parents arrived, they surveyed the destruction, then put their arms around their daughter and wrapped her in an embrace. "Oh, honey. I'm so sorry that this happened," her mother said.

Serenity clung tightly to her. "I don't understand any of this, Mom. I just don't understand."

"This is nothing but an act of Satan, trying to tear down the work of the ministry," her father said. "But that old devil will not prevail here. We are going to rebuild this place."

"It would take forever to fix this building," Serenity moaned. "It's almost completely wrecked. And I don't have the money to pay a contractor right now."

"*'O you of little faith,'*" her father chided her.

Serenity sighed in self-defeat. "I was in prayer about my ministry earlier this morning. Maybe this is God's way of telling me that what I'm doing isn't good enough."

Her mother took Serenity's face in her hands and turned her so that they were looking each other in the eye. "Now, you listen to me, Serenity Williams. The God I serve did not do this. You have been faithful to the Lord all your life, and you think this is how He would repay you for that?"

Serenity pulled away and put her hands on her hips. "You're right, Mom," she declared. "God didn't do this. Phillip's ex-wife did. And I'm going to make sure justice is done."

"That's fine, honey, but, right now, we are going to take this to God in prayer," her father said.

Nodding, Serenity said, "All right, Daddy." She called all of the crew members together, and they joined hands to battle in the Spirit.

Sixteen

SERENITY WAS STILL DISTRAUGHT THE NEXT DAY, BUT she converted her anger into effort as she worked alongside her crew and family members to clean up the studio. She crouched down to pick up a chunk of drywall, and as she stood up to carry it to one of the dumpsters, Phillip walked in. He was dressed in sweats, like everybody else, as if he'd come there to work. Serenity was caught off guard by his presence, and she didn't take a moment to think; she just ran over and wrapped her arms around him without caring who saw them or what they might think. At this moment, the sight of Phillip McKnight was precious to her.

When she released him, Phillip smiled and said, "I think I'll go outside and come back in again. I like the way you greet your workers."

"Don't tease me, Phillip. I've been so upset. I'm happy to see you, though."

"What happened, honey?"

She couldn't believe he was playing ignorant. She stepped back from him and put her hands on her hips. "You know what happened. Chantel destroyed my studio. I don't know what you told that woman, but it sure set her off."

"I haven't said anything to Chantel. What are you talking about?"

"I'm talking about the e-mail Chantel sent to me yesterday, telling me that I would pay for stealing your heart. Then, I get to work and find my studio totally trashed."

Phillip looked around at the destruction before him. "I hope Chantel didn't have anything to do with this. But, regardless of what someone I have no control over may or may not have done, I'm here to help. I hope you won't send me away again."

She wanted to tell Phillip not to unpack his bags and to get on the first plane back to Tampa. But her mouth wouldn't form the words.

Jay walked over with a paintbrush and handed it to Phillip. "Come on, McKnight! Enough sucking up to the boss. Get to work."

Phillip smiled as he took the brush. "Jay, man, I didn't know you would be here!"

"Yeah, my mom called me and said, 'The Saints may not need you right now, but your sister sure does.' So, I took a red-eye in last night."

"The Three Stooges are back together," Larry said as he and Monroe walked over. Larry was handling a broom, and Monroe held a trash bag.

"I guess we're going to be The Four Stooges today," Phillip said. "Let's get this place put back together."

After Phillip and her brothers got to work, Serenity's mother came up to her and said, "That was nice of Phillip to come and help us out, wasn't it?"

"Yes, it was, but I didn't ask you to call him."

Her mother held up her hands. "I didn't call him; Larry did. He was trying to raise money to help get this place fixed for you. So far, he's gotten donations from Jay, Monroe, your father and me, Melinda and Steven Marks, and Phillip."

Serenity put her hand to her mouth. When she removed it, she said, "Larry asked Phillip for money?"

"Girl, Phillip is a part of the body of Christ, same as you are. So, the same Spirit that caused you to help him with his building fund caused him to donate toward rebuilding your studio."

Her mother always told it like it was and got right to the point. Serenity could say nothing but ouch and amen. So, she gave her a hug, then returned to the group and got back to work.

That evening, when almost everyone had left, Serenity and Phillip sat on the floor eating Chicago dogs and potato chips while Jay talked on his cell phone. As Serenity's parents put away their paintbrushes, her mother said, "See you in the morning, sweetie. We need to go rest our bones."

Serenity got up off the floor and helped her mother with her coat, since her dad seemed to be struggling with his own. "You two look like a truck ran you over and then backed up and did it again. Please, stay home tomorrow. If I see either one of you in this place, I'm calling the cops."

Her mother chuckled, then said, "Don't make me laugh; it hurts."

Serenity kissed her mother on the cheek. As she leaned up to give her father a kiss, she whispered in his ear, "Please keep her away from here tomorrow, Daddy."

He glanced at his wife and then gave Serenity a nod.

"Does that go for me, too?" Jay asked, shutting his cell phone. "Should I stay home tomorrow?"

"If you're not here at eight in the morning, I'm going to send Paris Barnes to get you." Paris was a member of New Hope Church, and she'd been in love with Jay since they'd been ten-year-olds. But Jay had run like Forrest Gump every time she'd gotten close.

Holding up his hands, Jay said, "I'll be here before eight; just don't let Paris know that I'm in town."

Serenity playfully hit her brother in the arm. "Paris isn't thinking about you anymore, anyway. She's getting ready to marry Joe Milner."

"Joe Milner is a loser. Paris could do much better," Jay said.

"What do you care? You don't want her, right?"

"That's right," Jay said as he pulled his car keys out of his pocket. He dialed another number on his cell phone, then walked out of the studio.

Serenity sat back down next to Phillip and shook her head. "That cell phone is practically glued to Jay's ear."

"He's still young. He'll figure out what's best for him soon enough."

"I'm afraid it's going to be too late by the time he figures it out," Serenity said.

Phillip took a sip of his Pepsi, then asked, "What are you saying? You think this Paris girl is the right person for him?"

Nodding, Serenity took of sip of her lemonade.

"Well, what are you going to do about it?"

"What can I do? If Jay doesn't realize that he let the best woman he could ever have get away, then I can't help him." Serenity shrugged. "Besides, I don't understand men at all. For all I know, I could be pushing Jay toward someone he would be totally unhappy with."

Phillip stood up. "Come on, let's get out of here. If I have to be back by eight in the morning, I'm going to need some rest."

"Where are you staying?" Serenity asked as she accepted the hand he offered and stood up, too.

"Your parents are putting me up while I'm in town. Is there anything else you need done before we call it a night?"

"No, I can't lift another finger right now. But thanks." They put on their coats and headed toward the door. Serenity was feeling bad because of the way she had talked to Phillip when he'd first arrived. He had worked just as hard as everyone else, even after she'd blamed him for the damages. She stopped walking and touched Phillip's arm. "I'm sorry about what I said earlier. I know that you can't control the things Chantel does."

"Chantel is at home with a sprained ankle, so I doubt that she came to Chicago. If she is responsible, she must have paid someone to do this."

"Why would she do something like this to me? I don't even know her."

"You're asking the wrong person. Just as you don't understand men, I don't understand women."

Serenity wondered if Phillip wasn't just talking about his ex-wife. Was he sending her a jab, as well? She knew that her behavior toward him had been odd and unpredictable. One moment, she liked him; the next moment, she didn't want to be anywhere near him. But she'd never had to deal with anything like this before. She liked to watch drama on television; she'd never wanted to be mixed up in it. Wanting to clear the air, she said, "I know my behavior has probably been confusing, but it's not you. I really do care about you, Phillip. It's just that I want a drama-free life, and I don't think I'll get that with you."

❧

Phillip wanted to plead his case, but he knew now wasn't the right time. After all, his psycho ex-wife might have been responsible for all the damage to Serenity's studio. But, even as he prayed that Chantel had nothing to do with this, he remembered how angry she had been about his relationship with Serenity. So, he just took Serenity's hand in his and walked her to her car. A light snow had fallen during the day, and he used her ice scraper to brush the accumulation from her windows. Then, he stood and waited until she drove off before getting into his rental car and driving to the Williams' house.

As soon as he walked in the house, Lady Evelyn offered to make him some hot chocolate.

"That sounds like a plan. It is cold in the Midwest," Phillip said, rubbing his hands together.

"I'm surprised you know how to drive in the snow, being a Southern boy and all," Bishop Williams said.

"I've never liked the idea of having a driver, and when I played football, we were on the road so much that I had to learn to handle all types of road conditions."

"How was Serenity when you left the studio?" Lady Evelyn asked him.

"She seemed okay. I walked her to her car and waited until she drove off, and I called her before coming in the house. She's at home, safe and sound."

"You're a good man, Phillip McKnight," Lady Evelyn said as she handed him a mug of hot chocolate.

"Tell that to your daughter," Phillip said with a wry smile. He sat down at the kitchen table across from Bishop Williams.

"You don't want us to say anything, trust me," the Bishop said. "She'll never believe it if it comes from Mom and Dad. If you think you're working hard now to get that girl to come around, it will be ten times worse if Evelyn puts in a good word for you," he added with a chuckle.

"Lawrence, our daughter isn't like that," Lady Evelyn protested. "Besides, I already told her that I like Phillip."

"And look where that got him," her husband said, then took a sip of his hot chocolate.

Phillip hadn't been making much progress with Serenity, and he realized that Bishop Williams might be on to something. So, he said, "If it's all the same to you, Lady Evelyn, you don't need to tell Serenity how wonderful you think I am. Maybe, next time, you should tell her that I'm the biggest loser you ever met."

Lady Evelyn rolled her eyes. "Men," she muttered to herself, then walked out of the kitchen, shaking her head.

"Now, see what you've done?" Bishop Williams said.

"I just agreed with you, sir."

"Yes, and now my wife is mad." Bishop Williams stood up, smiling conspiratorially. "I guess I'd better go and make things right."

Phillip watched as Bishop Williams left the room, walking as if his destination mattered. Forty years of marriage, and the man was still in love as ever with his wife. Phillip wanted that kind of love for himself. He wanted that with Serenity. But he wasn't sure if he could make her want it with him. He took his cup to the sink and rinsed it out. When he turned to leave the kitchen, Lady Evelyn was back.

"Let me show you to your room."

"Thanks. I'm definitely ready to lay my head on a pillow."

As he followed Lady Evelyn up the stairs, she told him, "If Jay wasn't here, I'd let you stay in his room, where all the football paraphernalia is. But I think you'll be comfortable in the guest room."

"All I need is a bed, and I'll be set."

Once Phillip closed the door to the guest bedroom, he pulled out his cell phone and dialed three digits before hanging up. He had wanted to call Chantel and ask if she'd had anything to do with destroying Serenity's studio. Knowing that Chantel craved attention, however, he feared she might misconstrue the meaning of his phone call, and then she'd assault him with calls for weeks before getting the message that he didn't want to be bothered. So, Phillip put the phone down and decided to let the cops do their job.

He climbed into bed, laid his head on the pillow, said a quick prayer, and then drifted into the land of sleep. By morning, Phillip was well rested. He jumped in the shower, put on another pair of sweats, and then headed downstairs.

He followed his nose all the way to the kitchen, where Lady Evelyn was standing at the stove, flipping pancakes. Bishop Williams and Jay were seated at the table, reading the morning newspaper. Phillip looked at his watch and saw that it was ten minutes till seven. "How early do you people get up?"

"I was out all night," Jay said without an ounce of shame in his tone, "but these two have always been early risers."

Phillip turned to Lady Evelyn and said, "That food smells good—I hope you fixed enough for a hungry guest."

"I sure did. You and Jay need to have a hearty breakfast—you have a lot of work to get done today. Lawrence and I won't be there. We're going furniture shopping to replace the pieces that were damaged."

Phillip sat down. "Do you need any more money?"

Bishop Williams waved away his question. "You've done plenty already. We've paid for the supplies with the money Larry collected, and we have enough left for furniture." He glanced over at Lady Evelyn and added, "Since I've got the best shopper in the world with me, we may even be able to order more hoagies with the remaining money."

"That's great," Phillip said. "As long as you have enough to get Serenity everything she needs."

"Man, what gives with you?" Jay asked with a look of confusion on his face.

"What do you mean?" Phillip replied.

"Well, let me break it down for you," Jay said. "From what I heard, Serenity hadn't been your lady for a full day before she told you she didn't want to see you. And, now, you're throwing money in the hat and helping her repair her studio like some sucka'. This is not the Phillip McKnight I played ball with. What happened to you, brother?"

"Hush up, Jay. Phillip cares about your sister, and it's none of your business," Lady Evelyn said, coming to his defense.

"But the boy has gotten soft, Mama. I'm just wondering if he needs me to take him out on the field and help him man-up."

Lady Evelyn set platters of pancakes, sausage, bacon, and eggs on the table. "Hush your mouth and eat up," she said.

What could Phillip say? Jay had nailed him. As far as Phillip was concerned, he had gotten "soft" when he'd given his life to Christ, and his heart had softened yet again when he'd met Serenity. He didn't see anything wrong with that. But since Jay was also right about Serenity dumping him just hours after he'd asked to date her, he couldn't argue him on that point, either.

Maybe deflection would work. After Phillip loaded his plate with three pancakes, two sausage links, two strips of bacon, and a scoop of eggs, he looked directly at Jay and said, "I heard Paris Barnes is really happy with that Joe Milner guy. Did you get an invitation to the wedding?"

Seventeen

PHILLIP KNEW HE SHOULDN'T HAVE RETALIATED against Jay's teasing, but he couldn't help himself. When he saw the look of regret on Jay's face, he immediately felt bad. "I shouldn't have said that, Jay. Sorry about that."

Jay waved off his apology. "You didn't say anything wrong. Everybody knows I'm not interested in Paris. But everybody here also knows that Serenity dumped you." Jay laughed as he filled his plate.

"Do I need to call a time-out?" Bishop Williams asked.

"I'm not worried about Jay," Phillip said, then concentrated on the food on his plate.

When they were finished eating, Jay stood up and asked Phillip, "Can I catch a ride to the studio with you? I don't want to take Dad's car since I'm flying out today."

"Not a problem," Phillip said. "Let's get going."

For the duration of the drive to the studio, Jay kept messing with him. It went from cracks about Serenity to cracks about his age. "You'd better be glad you already retired, old man, because the Saints would have put a whupping on you this year."

"Talk to me when you have two Super Bowl rings. Until then, you are nothing more than a peasant to me." Phillip could trash-talk with the best of them. He'd learned his lessons on the football field and in the locker room.

Football players could be merciless to rookies. When he'd first joined an NFL team, he had sometimes thought he was playing against his own teammates rather than with them. The older players would try to take his head off during scrimmages, but what they'd meant for evil, God had turned to his favor. He'd become harder and stronger; he'd started scoring runs and touchdowns. His teammates had shown him respect then, but the trash talk had never stopped.

"All right, then, you're the big dog in this car. But, just remember, I'm only twenty-nine, so I have plenty of years ahead. I just may end up with three Super Bowl rings before I'm finished."

"Boy, please. With the way you fumble the ball, you're lucky you got even one Super Bowl ring."

Jay held up his fist, then said, "You'd just better worry about all this fumbling you're doing with my sister."

"Shut up, Jay," Phillip said as he pulled the car into the studio parking lot.

By noon, the place was starting to resemble what it once had been. "It's looking good, isn't it?" Phillip asked Serenity while they were taking a brief break.

With a tear trickling down her cheek, she said, "When I walked in here a couple of days ago, I thought we were going off the air for good. I knew I didn't have the money to get this place repaired fast enough to keep my time slot. But God is awesome. I can hardly believe how good this place is beginning to look again."

Just then, the door to the studio opened, and Detective Roundtree stepped in. "You're making progress, I see," he said as he approached Serenity and Phillip.

"Yes, sir," Serenity said, sniffling and then giving him a broad smile.

"I stopped by to tell you that the Tampa police questioned Chantel McKnight. She hasn't left Tampa in months. She's got a sprained ankle, and she's on crutches right now." Roundtree turned to Phillip and said, "Your ex-wife said that you could verify her alibi regarding when she sprained her ankle."

"Yes, it happened about a week ago. I took her to the hospital."

Roundtree turned back to Serenity. "So, I'm sure she wasn't part of the team who destroyed this place."

"She could have hired someone, though," Serenity pointed out.

"We're checking into that. I've also increased the police presence around the studio, so you should see police vehicles driving by more frequently for the next few weeks."

"Will that really do any good at this point? The damage has already been done; I doubt the perps will come back anytime soon," Phillip said.

"Criminals often return to the scene of the crime. They might pass by just to see how much time it takes to get this place back in order." Roundtree hunched his shoulders. "I don't really understand criminals' minds; I just hunt them down."

"Please, catch this maniac, and quick," Phillip said.

Serenity extended her hand to Roundtree. "Thank you for coming here with the update."

"Not a problem. I just wish I had better news to share."

Nodding, Serenity said, "Me, too."

After Roundtree left, Phillip picked up his paintbrush and resumed working alongside Monroe, painting the first wall that had been repaired completely. A few minutes later, Monroe stilled his paintbrush. "Can you believe him, coming in here dressed like *that*?"

Phillip stopped painting and followed Monroe's gaze to the studio entrance, where he saw Michael Randolph walking in. What was he doing here? He had on a brown, pin-striped suit, and he looked like he was getting ready to stand behind a pulpit and preach a sermon. With him were two men dressed in overalls and carrying toolboxes.

"I heard about what happened to your studio," he was telling Serenity, "so, I recruited two of my church members to help you get this place back in order."

Serenity shook hands with the two men and then said to Michael, "Thank you. I appreciate that you would do this for me."

Phillip and Monroe returned to their painting. "It's not like he's preaching somewhere in the middle of the afternoon on a Thursday," Monroe said, shaking his head. "He just didn't want anyone to ask him to lift a finger to help."

"It was nice of him to bring some people to pitch in, though," Phillip said, trying not to talk like a jealous jerk, which is how he felt.

"Well, you've got my vote," Monroe said, dipping his paintbrush in the can.

Phillip sighed. He figured that Monroe, like everyone else, knew that he was here with ulterior motives. But Michael probably had ulterior motives for showing up here today, too. At least Phillip was putting his muscle where his motives were.

Around two in the afternoon, Monroe left to take Jay to the airport. Larry left at four thirty, and the crew members began quitting at five. Once again, Phillip and Serenity were the last two workers on the site. Phillip looked at Serenity, who was sweeping up some debris with a broom. She looked ready for a break. "Why don't we get out of here and see a movie or something?" he suggested.

Serenity threw down the broom. "I would kill for some popcorn and a soft pretzel. Let's go."

Not only did Serenity get popcorn and a pretzel, but she got a hot dog and salted peanuts, too.

"Stocking up for the winter?" Phillip joked as they walked into the theater.

"Leave me alone. I've been working hard all day, and I'm hungry."

"You're right. You can pig out if you want." Phillip found two seats on the first level, and they sat down and gorged on popcorn, finishing most of it before the movie even began.

The Book of Eli was playing. The movie was intense, but Phillip loved every minute of it because he was with Serenity. She was different from the type of woman he'd dated in the past. Those women had been clingy and needy, and Phillip was able to admit that, at the time, he'd wanted his women to act that way. Fans, teammates, and coaches would cheer for him on the field, and he hadn't wanted the cheering to end, so he'd picked women who'd stroked his ego.

But when he'd come to know Jesus, suddenly, he no longer needed his ego stroked. That one simple yet profound decision had helped him to grow up in ways he'd never known were possible. He no longer needed clingy women, but he would have given anything for Serenity to cling to him like she had when he'd walked into her studio yesterday morning. He didn't understand her at all. Most women ran toward relationships, but Serenity seemed determined to keep her distance. Even the way she was seated right now spoke volumes to Phillip. She had her arms folded across her chest, rather than spread on the armrests; she looked wary, guarded. Obviously, she didn't want her arm to bump his.

After the movie, when they got in the car and started driving away from the theater, Phillip tried to hold Serenity's hand, but she pulled it away. "Have I done something wrong?"

"No, of course not, Phillip," she said, staring out the passenger window.

He tried again. "You seem a bit distant tonight. Does this have anything to do with Michael?"

"What Michael did today was nice, but he and I were never meant to be. I'm not interested in him, and he's not interested in me in that way, either."

Serenity might not be interested in Michael, but Phillip knew that Michael was definitely still interested in her. He was probably having second thoughts about letting her go. Too bad. Michael wasn't getting another chance, if Phillip had anything to say about it. "Look, Serenity. The only reason I asked is because I want to be in your life, but I need to know if you want to be in mine."

Serenity turned away from the window and looked at him. "You are the most wonderful man I have ever known, Phillip. I'm glad that I met you, because you've opened my eyes. Never again will I judge all men by the few who have left bad impressions on me."

"But that's not an answer to my question, Serenity. Do you want to be with me?"

Still avoiding the question, she asked, "How much longer will you be here?"

He decided to leave his unanswered question alone. "Well, we should be finished with the studio tomorrow, but I can stay for a few more days, if you need me to. I don't really have to get back to Tampa until a week from Sunday."

At the mention of *Sunday*, Serenity's eyes grew wide. "Oh, my goodness! With everything going on this week,

I completely forgot about your mortgage-burning celebration next weekend."

"Yeah, I really need to get back for that. I don't know if my congregation would forgive me if I missed it."

"You should have been in Tampa helping with the final preparations for this event, instead of here, helping me." She put her head in her hands and exhaled. "I'm so sorry, Phillip. I never should have let you stay."

"It's all right, Serenity. Derek has been handling everything. He's going to preach this Sunday, and then I'll go back and preach next Sunday for the celebration. Everything will be fine; don't worry about it."

"How do you know you can trust Derek? He might be trying to split up your church so he can start his own and have some instant members."

Phillip laughed.

But Serenity didn't sound amused. "I'm serious, Phillip. Ask Larry—he'll tell you how one of his elders stabbed him in the back."

Phillip shook his head. "I can't live my life being afraid of what might happen, Serenity. I'd rather trust people and let their word be good enough for me."

Shaking her head, Serenity said, "Good luck with that. I'd rather live my life by Ronald Reagan's motto: 'Trust, but verify.'"

Serenity had practically been born on a church pew—she'd grown up in ministry, and he hadn't. So, he knew that she had seen more treachery in church than he had. But Jesus had seen the same things. Judas sold Him out for a bag of silver, Peter denied Him three times, and, after His death, all His disciples went about their business, forgetting about the work that had been assigned to them. Jesus had known all those things would happen, yet He'd still chosen to be the Savior of traitorous humanity.

When Phillip pulled up in front of Serenity's condo and stopped the car, he turned to her and said, "You know, Jesus was betrayed, yet He forgave, and I would venture to say that He trusts each and every one of us, in our God-given missions, to forgive others and not assume that they'll betray us."

Serenity opened her mouth, as if to say something, but then she closed it, opened her door, and got out of the car. As she stood on the sidewalk, looking down at him, she said, "You shouldn't be here any longer. I want you to go home tomorrow." With that, she turned and headed up the walkway to her building.

Eighteen

WHEN SHE ARRIVED AT WORK THE NEXT DAY, SErenity was stunned to see that several furniture trucks were being unloaded. She looked at Pam and asked, "Where did all this stuff come from?"

"They said that your mom picked it out yesterday and demanded that they get it here first thing this morning."

Serenity laughed. Only Evelyn Williams would have been able to purchase all the furniture her studio needed in one single day. "I told that woman to get some rest. When she didn't show up here yesterday, I thought she was taking my advice."

"I've known your mother for only two years, and I knew better than that," Pam said with a grin.

"I guess you're right." Serenity put her arm around Pam's shoulder and said, "Well, it looks like we're back in business." Together, they walked into the studio and began showing the delivery people where to put the furniture.

Serenity couldn't believe how well everything was turning out. Her family and Phillip had really come through for her. At a time when she had been ready to throw in the towel, they'd stepped in and turned things around. She decided that from this day forward, she would no longer call her brothers The Three Stooges, because they weren't bumbling idiots; they were heroes, as far as she was concerned.

Serenity would have to find a way to thank Phillip, as well. He'd gone out of his way and left his church at a time when he was needed there. She would never forget him. But that didn't mean that she thought they should fall in love and build a life together. She looked at her wristwatch, noting that it was almost ten in the morning. Since he hadn't arrived yet, Serenity figured that he must have followed her orders and gone back to Tampa. Suddenly, she felt the need to be alone.

She went into her new office and sat down at her desk. She was a week behind schedule and really needed to catch up on some work, but there was no way she was going to get any of that done when she still needed to put her files back in order. She tapped her fingers on her desk, contemplating where to begin.

Just then, there was a knock, and her door opened. "Do you have a moment?" Pam asked, peeking in.

"Of course. I can't figure out where to begin, so I'm just kind of sitting here," Serenity said.

Pam walked in with a few files in her hand. "I just wanted to go over next week's schedule with you."

"How were our ratings this week?"

Pam averted her eyes. "We've all been busy with the cleanup and repairs, so I haven't had a chance to verify that my numbers are accurate."

"Just spill it, Pam. You know exactly what the ratings were, so tell me."

"Okay, we lost about a third of our viewers, but, hopefully, we'll get at least half of them back. We might even get some new viewers if we do a couple commercials announcing that we have all new shows coming up."

"How much will that cost us?" Serenity asked. She had been feeling good about their progress when she'd seen the furniture trucks that morning, but now it looked like they had taken a serious hit elsewhere.

"I'll check on the rates and get back to you."

"Thanks, Pam. What else do you have?"

"Well, I was thinking that we should thank all the people who chipped in and helped us get this studio back in working order."

"Yes, of course. I was planning to send thank-you notes to everyone."

Pam shook her head. "I think we should do it on the air."

"I don't want our viewers to know that someone vandalized the studio."

"It's public knowledge, Serenity. We reported this to the police, remember?"

"I know. I just don't feel comfortable talking about this on the air. I'm sure you'll come up with something else that's just as wonderful," Serenity assured her.

Pam lifted her hands and said, "All right, back to the drawing board."

"Things will work out for us, Pam. You'll see. God is not going to let the enemy have the victory."

"I hope you're right," Pam said as she opened the door to leave.

"Now, that's service," Serenity heard Michael say. He must have been just about to knock on the door.

"I wasn't trying to serve you, Pastor Randolph. I was just opening the door so I could get back to work." Pam looked back at Serenity and rolled her eyes, then turned and walked past Michael into the hallway.

"Do you have a moment, Serenity?" Michael asked as he stepped into her office.

"Well, you certainly look different today," she said, reacting to his overalls and baseball cap.

"I figured I could help get this place back in order," he said.

"The guys you brought yesterday to help should have told you that we're pretty much finished. There're only a few spots left to fix, and the new furniture is being unloaded right now."

"I've had a lot of back pain lately, but maybe I can help them bring in some of the pieces that aren't so heavy," Michael said, looking disappointed.

Serenity stood up and walked around to the front of her desk. "You don't have any meetings this morning?"

"I did, but I cancelled them."

She gawked at him.

"Don't look so shocked," Michael said as he moved closer to Serenity. "I've been thinking about the way things ended between us, and I owe you an apology."

"You don't owe me anything, Michael. Anyway, you were right. The two of us don't belong together; we were just holding on to something that never should have been in the first place."

"That's not true." Michael took her hands in his. "I've loved you for a long time, Serenity. I just let my pride get in the way. But, now, I realize that you and I should be building our ministry empire together, not separately."

Serenity snatched her hands away. "Are you nuts?" she asked. "You're engaged to Karen—or have you forgotten that?"

"I made a mistake with Karen. I never should have let you go. Please, listen to me, Serenity. You and I belong together."

Serenity backed away from Michael as she said, "Look, Phillip. I don't know what this is all about, but—"

"My name is not Phillip!" Michael shouted.

"What?"

"You just called me Phillip. How could you do that, Serenity? I mean, we've been apart for only a few months. Have you replaced me already?"

"We've been apart for more than eight months, Michael. And I apologize for calling you Phillip, but he has nothing to do with this."

"Nothing to do with what?" Phillip asked from the doorway of her office.

She whirled around to face him, feeling as if her heart was about to jump out of her body. "Phillip? I thought you were on your way back to Tampa."

"My flight doesn't leave for another few hours, and I wanted to check in with Detective Roundtree again."

"You went down to the police station?" Serenity asked.

"Sure did, and I have some good news," Phillip reported.

Serenity turned to Michael. "Would you give me and Phillip a moment to talk?"

Michael put his arm around her shoulders and said, "I'm sure Phillip won't have a problem sharing his information with both of us."

Serenity stepped away from Michael again, then turned back to Phillip. "What did Detective Roundtree say?"

Phillip looked from Serenity to Michael and then back at Serenity again. Putting his hands in his pockets, he said, "They caught one of the guys who vandalized the studio. He's in a gang, so Roundtree thinks that they'll take several members of that gang off the streets."

Michael picked up Serenity and swung her around as she wriggled and tried to protest. "That's great, honey! Thank God they caught those guys. I was so worried about you."

When Michael put her back down, she turned to Phillip, but he was no longer standing in the doorway. She rushed out of her office.

"Where are you going?" Michael called after her.

Serenity ignored him and looked around the studio for Phillip. By the time she spotted him, he was out the door. "Phillip, wait!" she yelled, running after him.

Phillip was opening his car door when Serenity stepped outside. "Wait!" she yelled again. But he started the car. Serenity knew he was going to pull away if she didn't do something to stop him, so she swung open the passenger door and jumped in. "Turn off the car, Phillip. Why are you leaving?"

"I have to get to the airport," he said without looking at her.

"I thought your plane didn't leave for several hours," Serenity said.

He pointed toward the studio. "Don't you need to get back in there?"

"I can't get my mind wrapped around work. I was sitting behind my desk, trying to figure out where to start first. So, I don't think I'm going to be any good in there right now."

"What about Michael? Don't you need to get back to him?"

"Look, Phillip. I know it looked bad, but I have no idea why Michael was acting like that today."

Phillip sighed, then looked over at her and asked, "Do you want to get a cup of coffee so we can talk about what Roundtree told me?"

"Yes, I would," Serenity said. She buckled her seat belt and leaned back in the passenger seat.

Phillip backed away from the studio and drove down the street to the local coffee shop Serenity had told him she frequented. They went in, ordered two coffees, and took a seat at a small table. After taking several sips of his coffee, Phillip finally broke the silence. "I was acting like a jealous idiot back there. Sorry about that."

Serenity put her hand over his. "You don't have anything to be sorry about. I know it looked bad, especially after I told you that I wasn't interested in Michael. And I'm not, Phillip. I just don't know why he came to the studio today, acting the way he did."

"Maybe his girlfriend broke up with him or something," Phillip said.

"He seemed really happy with Karen, so don't ask me. Remember, I'm the one who doesn't understand men at all."

Phillip laughed.

Serenity took a sip of her coffee. "Okay, let's get to it. Why did those guys ransack my studio, and how did Roundtree find them?"

"So far, he has only one of the gang members in custody. They caught him pawning some of your equipment. They also found more of your stuff in his apartment. But he has no idea why the gang chose to target your studio. Sometimes, gangs do things like this to initiate new members."

"Did Detective Roundtree ask the guy if Chantel paid him to trash my place?"

"He said he didn't know Chantel."

"But she e-mailed me the same day my studio was trashed. It had to be Chantel, Phillip. Doesn't that make sense to you?"

He held up a hand. "I'm not trying to defend Chantel, but I really don't think she did this."

"I can't understand how you feel so sure she isn't behind this stuff. She clearly has a problem with me."

"I can see Chantel sending threatening e-mails, but having someone slit your tires and vandalize your studio just doesn't seem like her style."

"Maybe you just don't want it to be Chantel because, then, you'd have to admit that your ex is crazy."

"You might be right about that. I don't think anyone wants to find out that he spent years married to a mental patient without knowing it." Phillip took another sip of his coffee. "Are you going to be okay?"

Serenity sighed. "I will be. I just don't know why they picked me. I try really hard not to bother other people, try not to provoke them, and then someone targets me for no reason. It just blows my mind."

"You can't shield yourself from life, Serenity. Sometimes, things just happen, even when we've done nothing to prevent or provoke them."

"Well, thanks for going down to the police station to check on the investigation."

"You don't need to thank me. I couldn't leave town without knowing where we stood."

Sometimes, Serenity couldn't believe how thoughtful Phillip was. He treated people with kindness and warmth. Before she could stop herself, she opened her mouth and blurted out, "Your ex-wife *must* be crazy; if you were mine, I'd never let you go."

"I wanted to be yours, Serenity. But you've let me go twice now."

Nineteen

BACK IN TAMPA, PHILLIP FOUND HIMSELF AT THE Raymond James Stadium, home to his beloved Tampa Bay Buccaneers. He'd played the first home game at this stadium on September 20, 1998. He and many of his teammates still relived that day as though it had been the Super Bowl, because they'd won a sensational victory against the Chicago Bears with a score of 27 to 15. Phillip loved football. He'd played it well, and he'd had some awesome teammates, many of whom he still kept up with. Derek had joined him on the church staff, and many Bucs, retired and current players alike, attended New Destiny.

The Raymond James Stadium had been home to him for so many years. He'd loved running the football down the field and looking up into the stands as the crowd cheered him on. But his favorite thing about this stadium was the 103-foot-long pirate ship harbored in the Buccaneer Cove. Each time one of the Bucs made a field goal or a touchdown, that ship would come alive with a cannon that fired as many times as the points scored—three for a field goal, six for a touchdown, with one or two additional shots for an extra point or a two-point conversion.

Phillip figured that the 24-foot by 92-foot, high-definition televisions were the fans' favorite things about the stadium, because they allowed them to see all of the action on the field, no matter where they were seated. But Phillip's favorite thing was definitely that pirate ship. He loved to hear those cannons fire.

From time to time, when he had something on his mind, he came to the stadium. He'd had some of his most productive prayer times just sitting in the stands, listening to the sound of crows cawing—a recording that was piped through the sound system when the stadium was empty to keep pigeons from roosting in the rafters. The sound of the birds made him feel closer to God and exhilarated his prayers. He felt that this was the place he needed to be in order to hear from God, because he truly needed to understand why he kept falling for women who wanted something else in life more than they wanted to be with him. Chantel had wanted the money more than she'd wanted to stay married to him. Serenity was not money-hungry like his ex-wife, but she had other issues that made her unavailable to him.

"Lord, why do I keep doing this to myself?" Phillip yelled the words so loud, they echoed through the stadium. "I didn't want to fall in love again; didn't want to experience this type of pain ever again. But here I am, Lord. And I need Your help." He leaned his head back and looked heavenward. "If Serenity is not the woman for me, then I need to release her from my heart, but I don't know how to do that." He continued pouring out his heart to God until tears were rolling down his cheeks. Feeling self-conscious, he wiped his face.

As he was composing himself, his cell phone rang. He quickly checked the caller ID, hoping that Serenity had decided she couldn't live without him, but it wasn't Serenity. "What's going on, Chantel?" he asked when he answered the phone.

"I could ask you the same thing. I've been calling you for days, and you haven't answered your phone. For all you knew, someone could have come into my house and killed me. I can't defend myself with this ankle."

Sighing heavily, Phillip said, "This is the last time I'm going to say this to you, Chantel, so I hope you understand exactly where I'm coming from this time. We are divorced. I am no longer responsible for what happens to you, and I need to move on with my life. So, please, stop calling me."

"You're just saying that because of that talk show host in Chicago. But when she goes back to that ex-fiancé of hers, you'll finally get the picture and come running back to me."

"Her name is Serenity, and she's more than a talk show host. She is a minister of the gospel. And I need you to leave her alone, too. I'm not dating her."

"Then, why did you spend this past week in Chicago helping her put her studio back together?"

He held the phone away from his ear, looked at it, and then put it back against his ear. "How do you know where I've been?"

"For one thing, the police asked me about the disturbance at that woman's studio. As if I would lower myself to do something like that!"

"I already told the police that I didn't think you had anything to do with it. But that doesn't answer my question. How did you know that I was in Chicago? I know the police didn't tell you."

She didn't answer.

"Who told you, Chantel?" Phillip demanded. He wanted to know who was telling his business to his ex-wife so that he could put a stop to it immediately. Chantel was the last person he wanted knowing his comings and go-ings. She didn't have that right anymore.

"It's not so hard to figure out where you're spending your time these days. What I don't understand is, why her? I mean, she's pretty, but she's not beautiful, and you like beautiful women, Phillip. That's always been your weakness."

"I've got to go, Chantel."

"Wait, don't hang up. I need to know something."

"What is it?" he asked, quickly losing patience with her.

"I don't understand why you don't want me back. You begged me not to divorce you. You claimed you wanted to stay married; I'm offering you that. We can get back together anytime you want, but now, suddenly, things have changed. If that woman in Chicago is not the rea-son, then, what is?"

Phillip had wanted to stay married because he hadn't wanted to have the stigma of being a divorced pastor. If Chantel had listened to him, he would have stayed married to her forever and never thought twice about it. But, now, he realized that he would have been miserable married to her. She was not the woman for him, and he thanked God that he had been able to see the truth. "We are not right for each other, Chantel. My life is about serv-ing God and ministering to people, and you want nothing to do with any of that."

"I don't need to be involved in your ministry for us to be together."

"Yes, you do. Any wife of mine has to be involved in my ministry. Besides, you'd soon grow bored and find another Chad. So, please don't call me anymore, Chantel. This is good-bye." With that, Phillip ended the call.

Feeling refreshed, he stood up and jogged down the steps of the stadium. God had given him an answer to his dilemma with Serenity through his conversation with Chantel. He had just told Chantel that a wife of his had to be involved in his ministry. Serenity didn't want to be involved in his ministry. So, he needed to let her go and wait on the Lord to send the woman He had for him.

He drove to the church, where he would force himself to concentrate on his own business. Before getting to work, though, he went to Derek's office and knocked on the door.

"Come in," Derek said.

Phillip opened the door and said, "Hey, just wanted to let you know that I'm back."

Derek smiled. "I didn't think we would see you until Sunday or Monday."

"I left early. I'm going to check my e-mails and do a bit of catch-up work before I go home. Why are you still here? It's six o'clock on a Friday night."

"My boss has been missing in action, so I've been doing double duty around here."

"Derek, I appreciate what you did for me, but I'm back now, and I won't be running off to Chicago anytime soon."

Derek stood up and stretched. "So, does this mean that your damsel in distress has been rescued?"

"Yeah, we were able to get her studio back in working order. And the police found one of the guys who vandalized the building. He's in a gang, so they think it was part of some initiation."

"I'm just glad you were able to help her."

"Now I need to work on my sermon. I've been so busy helping Serenity that I haven't had time to even think about what I'm going to say at the celebration."

"Well, you've got until next Sunday to figure it out. Do you still want me to preach this Sunday?"

"I would appreciate it. I'm too brain-dead to attempt a sermon right now."

Derek laughed as he grabbed his keys off his desk. "Yeah, you would probably preach about shopping again."

"Whatever," Phillip said with a half smile.

"Well, I'm out."

"All right, I'll see you later," Phillip said as he headed to his office.

"Hey, Phillip," Derek called after him.

"Yeah?" He turned to face his friend.

"Are you okay?"

Phillip shook his head. "I'm not going to lie, man. I could use some prayer right now."

"Ah, dawg, I'm ready to go home, and now I've got to stay here with you?"

Phillip could tell that Derek wasn't really upset, so he said, "Look, if you don't want to stay here and pray me off the ledge, don't worry about it. Just don't act surprised when you get the news that I've jumped."

"Why don't you go put on some sweats and meet me in the fitness room?" Derek told him.

A few minutes later, when the two men were pumping iron, Derek asked, "You've got it bad for this one, don't you?"

Lying down on the bench press, Phillip completed his first set, then stood up and said, "I can't stop thinking about her. I've fallen in love with this woman, and she doesn't want anything to do with me."

"Did she tell you that she didn't want anything to do with you?" Derek asked, starting a set on the bench press.

"Not in those exact words, but she got her point across when she kept telling me to go back to Tampa."

"She looked like she enjoyed your company the last time she was here. What happened?"

"Serenity's past isn't like ours. We gave our lives to the Lord after running the streets and doing anything and everything we wanted to. She's been in church all of her life—on the inside, too, as a bishop's daughter. She's seen things that have caused her to not want to pastor a church. So, dating someone like me scares her, because she doesn't even want to marry a pastor."

"I don't get that—isn't she a preacher, herself?" Derek said.

"She's an evangelist, which is very different from what we do. In her capacity as a Christian talk show host, she is able to touch lives without allowing the people to touch her. And that's the way she likes it."

"Wow, that's deep."

"Tell me about it," Phillip said. "So, anyway, I think it's best that I leave her alone."

"And you can turn your feelings on and off, just like that?" Derek asked skeptically.

"What choice do I have? The woman has issues with pastors. I don't see myself changing professions anytime soon, and I would want my lady involved in the ministry with me. Serenity doesn't want that, and we both know that I've already tried to force a woman into wanting what I want. That didn't turn out so well, so I'm not about to go down that road again."

Twenty

SERENITY FELT LIKE A WALKING ZOMBIE. EVERY DAY, she went into work, filmed her segment, and then went home again and munched on potato chips, buttered popcorn, chocolate bars, and whatever else she could get her hands on, all while watching a sappy romance movie. She kept a box of tissues next to the couch, because the scenes in which the guy finally gets the girl always caused a river of tears to cascade down her face.

As she got ready for bed, she would try to pray her feelings of loneliness away, but, each morning, as she opened her eyes to greet the new day, she would feel the stinging pain right in the center of her heart. "Take it away, Lord, take it away," she kept praying.

The effort of getting out of bed was like lifting a car off her chest. She wanted to pull the covers over her head and spend the day slumbering in blessed quietness. But she had obligations to fulfill. She had a camera crew and a staff of people who depended on her to do her job so that they could keep theirs. Not to mention that her life was about ministry, and if she was stuck in bed, she wasn't ministering to anyone, not even her own lovesick heart.

After about a week of this, Pam greeted her one morning with a cup of coffee when she walked into the studio. "How are you doing today?" she asked.

"I'm okay," said Serenity. "Why, is something wrong?"

"No, no, no," Pam assured her. "I just wanted to make sure that you got some rest last night so that you can be at your best when you interview our guest today."

"I get it—you don't think the interview with Dr. Black was handled right. Why didn't you just tell me that yesterday, instead of plying me with coffee and badgering me as soon as I walk through the door?" Serenity heard the sound of her voice and could tell that she was not being polite at all. She stopped walking and looked directly at Pam. "I'm sorry; I shouldn't have said that to you."

Pam grabbed Serenity's arm and directed her to her office. "Have a seat, hon."

"I'm just tired, Pam. I've been staying up late watching movies. I won't do it again, and I promise I will try to be a livelier interviewer."

"That's all I'm trying to say, Serenity. The people you interview deserve your full attention. Maybe I pushed you to go live again too soon after everything that happened to the studio. If you want me to cancel the rest of the interviews this week and just start back fresh next week, I'll do it."

"No, that's not fair to our guests, either. Don't worry about me; I'll make it work."

"Okay, you've got an hour before you're needed in makeup, so you might want to review the list of questions that Pastor Delores Right's people sent over." Pam handed Serenity a sheet of paper, then left her alone.

Serenity took a sip of her coffee and then looked over the bio and question sheet for her guest. She'd met Pastor Delores a couple of years ago at a conference where they both were speaking. The woman had seemed pleasant, and, as Serenity had listened to her message, she'd known that she wanted to introduce this woman of God to her viewing audience. But Serenity knew that she was not in the right frame of mind to help Pastor Delores get her message across. She picked up her phone and dialed Pam's extension. When Pam picked up, she said, "Can you call Pastor Delores's church and see if they can email an mp3 file of one of her best messages?"

"Sure—do you want to plug bits and pieces of that into the segment?"

"No, I want to introduce Pastor Delores and then let the viewers see her in action. Let her sermon roll for about twenty minutes, and then I'll let her close out the show."

"We won't have time to edit the sermon to fit it into that twenty-minute spot," Pam said.

"That's okay. Just let it roll for twenty minutes and then cut it off."

There was silence on the line. Finally, Pam said, "Okay—if that's what you want, I'll make it happen."

Serenity knew it wasn't the right way to handle the segment, but Pastor Delores could preach like Jackie Mc-Cullough. Her viewers would be in for the treat of a lifetime, even if they saw only twenty minutes of the message.

She put the list of questions on her desk and then picked up the phone and dialed Melinda's number. "Hey! How's everything going with the family?" she said when Melinda picked up.

"Serenity? Hey, girl! What are you doing calling me right now? You're normally too busy getting ready for your show to talk."

"I need to know how my godchild is doing, don't I?"

"Your godchild is getting on my nerves. I'm having morning, noon, and nighttime sickness right now, so you better ask me about this when the nausea goes away."

"My mom was sick like that with me, but not with any of my brothers. So, you, my dear friend, are most likely having a girl."

"Listen to you, making baby predictions when you should be working. So, what gives, Serenity? And don't say 'Nothing,' because I saw the show yesterday; you looked like you'd rather be anywhere but there. Or, should I say, you'd rather be in Tampa?"

"I don't know what's wrong with me, Melinda. I'm in no mood to do my job. I'm supposed to interview Pastor Delores Right today, but I'm so afraid I'm going to botch the interview that I'm just going to show one of her ministry tapes for most of the segment."

"Well, if you're in the same mood you were in yesterday, I'd say you made a wise decision. Just don't beat yourself up about this, Serenity. If you remember, I came to stay with you when I was struggling with my feelings for Steven. So, if you need a place to lie low, you can always come to Baltimore."

"Yeah, I remember how you came here, claiming you wanted to work at my studio, and all you did was sit in the audience and listen to Yvonne Milner's interview."

"I'm not ashamed of skipping out on work that day. God had me in the right place at the right time. And, you know what? That's exactly what I'm going to pray for on your behalf—God's perfect timing."

⟡

Phillip was in need of prayer. He was getting his butt kicked on the field. The guys had decided on a Thursday night scrimmage. Derek had suggested the idea as a way to pull him out of the cloud of despair he'd fallen into this past week. But Phillip had made more fumbles than ever before. He should have been sidelined an hour ago.

"Man, you are sorry. What's up with you?" one of his teammates yelled from across the field.

"You can't be a superhero every time out. Sometimes, the other team is going to score," Phillip said, trying to justify his poor showing.

"Yeah, but when are *we* gonna score?" another teammate asked.

Phillip threw the ball down. "Look, if you guys don't want me out here, I can go home. I have plenty of better things to do than take this kind of abuse."

He started walking off the field, but Derek ran after him. "Come on, Phillip. You know those guys didn't mean anything by that."

"Yes, we did," came a yell from the field.

"See, they don't want me here," Phillip said.

"They just don't think you're focused on the game. Let someone else be quarterback, and you can play another position."

"Yeah, you're right. I'm not focused enough to call the plays. Let Lenny be the quarterback tonight, and I'll sit out for a little while."

"But you're going to get back in the game, right?" Derek asked as he headed back to the field.

"I need a little time. I'll be the cheerleader for a little while," Phillip said with a forced smile.

He ended up watching the rest of the game from the sidelines, rooting for his team as they made a couple of touchdowns. Even though they lost, they didn't get clobbered, as he was sure they would have if he'd stayed in the game.

When the game was over, Phillip jumped in his car and headed to a sub shop. He needed a cheesesteak like he needed to breathe. He ordered two, just in case he got hungry in the middle of the night. He jumped back in his car and was heading home when he remembered that he didn't have anything to drink. So, he pulled into the mini-mart a few blocks from his house and purchased a few two-liters. As he got back in the car, he noticed that the same dark sedan he'd seen at the park and at the sub shop was also parked at the mini-mart.

As he searched his memory, he recalled seeing this same car near the church parking lot and other places he'd gone throughout the week. He got back out of his car and approached the vehicle warily. The man behind the wheel rolled down his window, as if he'd been expecting Phillip to come talk to him.

"Who are you, and why are you following me?" Phillip asked.

"My name is Dan Truman, but I'm not following you," the man said. "I'm not sure why you'd think that."

"Don't play games with me," Phillip said. "I've seen you several times, and not just today, either. I just didn't bother to put two and two together until tonight."

The man hunched his shoulders.

"Did Chantel put you up to this?"

"Sir, I'm not following you. I'm sorry if our paths seem to have been crossing a lot lately."

Phillip wasn't crazy. He knew exactly what was going on. He'd caught her. "You were following me in Chicago, also, weren't you? That's how Chantel knew what I was doing."

The man didn't say anything.

"Tell Chantel that if she keeps this up, I will press charges against her and file for a restraining order. I don't want to see you again. Do I make myself clear?" Phillip asked.

"Perfectly," the man said, then drove off.

As he headed home, Phillip felt a freedom he hadn't known in quite some time. This was it for him and Chantel; he could feel it. The Lord was releasing him from her grip. But he'd also meant what he'd said. If Chantel persisted in pursuing him, he would file for a restraining order.

When he got home, he sat down at the kitchen table and started into one of his sub sandwiches, all the while pondering his situation. He was free from Chantel, but did he also need to face the fact that he was free from Serenity?

Before he could contemplate the thought much longer, his phone rang. he saw that it was Derek, and he picked up. "What? You called to gloat about winning the game?"

"No, I called to do you a favor, my man."

"What's that?"

"Missy says I should stay out of it and let you and Serenity work things out, but I can't stand seeing you like this. So, I've set you up on a blind date."

"You did what?" Phillip couldn't help letting his annoyance show. In all his years of dating, he had never needed a friend to fix him up. He wasn't even sure if he wanted to date anyone other than Serenity, anyway.

"You heard me; it's time you moved on and got your life back. You've been away from Chicago since last Friday. Tomorrow, it will have been a full week. Has Serenity called you once since you've been back in Tampa?"

"No," Phillip admitted.

"Then, why not give Denise a chance? She seems like a real nice woman. Even Missy thinks so."

"I thought Missy told you to mind your own business."

"She did, but right before that, she said that Denise seemed like she could be the right woman for you. Just give her a chance, Phillip. I checked her out. Denise is not a gold digger, and she doesn't have a problem with preachers."

"But is she a Christian?" Phillip asked. That was his most important criterion.

"Now, you know I wouldn't set you up with a woman who wasn't devoted to the Lord," Derek said.

"Well, thanks for thinking of me, but I don't think it would be fair to go out with Denise while I'm still thinking about Serenity."

"And just how do you think you're going to get over Serenity if you don't get back on the dating scene?" Derek asked him.

"I don't know, my friend. I guess that's something I need to pray about," Phillip said.

After their phone conversation, Phillip finished his sub, put the second one in the fridge for later, and headed upstairs. As he got ready for bed, he wondered if his call from Derek had been God's way of telling him that he was free from Serenity and needed to move on with his life. Maybe he'd give Denise a chance, after all.

Twenty-one

SERENITY WAS LOST. SHE WAS HOPELESSLY IN LOVE WITH a man who was all wrong for her. She knew from the minute that Pam had suggested doing the interview with Phillip McKnight that no good would come from it, but she had been so bitter toward male preachers because of Michael that she had agreed to participate in the interview, hoping that she would be able to expose the preacher to the world as an egomaniac. Instead, she'd let Phillip get too close to her heart, and now she was paying the price—yet again—for falling in love with a pastor.

She'd thought that once he left town, things would go back to normal, and she would be able to focus on her work again. Yet, she couldn't wrap her mind around anything but him and the pain she felt at his absence. Why was she feeling this way? Phillip was not her type. If she had learned nothing else from her failed engagement to Michael, it was that she didn't want to marry a preacher. They were too self-centered and couldn't abide with her popularity, especially when it exceeded theirs. Plus, they expected their wives to be involved in their ministries and to interact closely with their parishioners—definitely the last thing Serenity wanted to do. It was because of those reasons that Michael had called off their wedding.

The same thing would probably happen with Phillip. Even though Serenity knew in her heart that he would be patient with her, his patience would eventually run out. Then, he, too, would expect her to give up her television show and devote herself to the duties of a pastor's wife, a first lady of a church, and a mother. But she couldn't do it. She didn't want the responsibility that her mother had with the congregation of New Hope Church. She didn't want to become so closely connected to people that it broke her heart when they left the church or disappointed her. Ratings were one thing; church members were another thing altogether.

Phillip had looked so disappointed when he'd left last week, as if his hopes and dreams had been crushed, and he no longer believed in fairy-tale endings. If there was anyone with whom Serenity would have wanted to live happily ever after, it would have been Phillip. But life hadn't turned out the way Serenity had expected, and she knew firsthand that some prayers received answers that were far from her personal desires. Serenity wiped away the tears tolling down her face, then laid her head on her desk and continued to lament over the prospect of a life without Phillip.

When a knock sounded on her office door, Serenity lifted her head. The door opened, and her mother peeked inside.

"Hey, sweetie! I saw that your car was still outside, so I figured I'd come check on you," she said as she entered the office.

"Hi, Mom," Serenity said blandly, then lowered her head back down on the desk.

"What's wrong, honey? I've been calling you for hours, but I keep getting your voice mail right away."

"I need to recharge the battery," Serenity mumbled.

"Looks like you need to recharge your own battery. If you're too tired to work, just go on home. It's almost five o'clock, anyway."

Serenity sat up and confessed, "I'm not tired, Mom. I miss Phillip."

"Well, you ought to. It's your own fault that Phillip is gone. I wouldn't be surprised if he never came back to Chicago again."

"Mom, you're supposed to be on my side!" she whined. "Besides, you don't know anything about what happened."

"Oh, yes, I do. I saw the look on Phillip's face when he walked into the house last week. He didn't say anything to me about it, but I heard him tell your father that you'd told him to leave."

"He belongs in Tampa, Mother. While he was up here trying to help me, that elder friend of his was probably stealing church members away."

Shaking her head, her mother sat down. "Your dad asked me to stay out of this and let you figure things out on your own, but I just can't stand by and watch you destroy yourself over things you've never understood."

"What things?"

"For some reason, you've got it in your head that Pastor Matthew went behind your father's back and started a new church."

"Yep, and stole his members as he walked out the door, just like Mark Sampson did to Larry."

"Okay, I agree with you about Mark Sampson. He did start his church behind Larry's back and then stole half the members. But Larry was able to forgive Mark and move on. Now, Larry's ministry has grown threefold since that happened, and Pastor Sampson is still trying to find enough members to fill up his storefront church."

"But that doesn't excuse what he did, and neither does it excuse what Pastor Matthew did to Daddy. In case you hadn't noticed, Mom, Pastor Matthew's church is doing just fine. He even has more members than Daddy does."

"Yes, and your father mentored Pastor Matthew and brags about his success every chance he gets. Why do you think he still attends our dinner parties, and our two churches fellowship together whenever we can?"

"Because Daddy has a forgiving heart. I just don't know if I could be that forgiving, Mom. That's why I don't want the responsibility of leading a church—or being married to someone who does." Serenity wiped another tear from her cheek. "And, since I don't want that kind of responsibility, it's foolish to even entertain the thought of being with Phillip."

"Michael is a pastor, too, Serenity, and you were engaged to marry him. So, what's the difference?"

"I didn't want anything to do with Michael's church, either. He thought I would change my mind, but when he realized that I wouldn't, and when my ministry made me more widely known than him, he began to resent me. Michael said I was selfish and cared only about my own growth in ministry—which isn't true."

"Michael and Phillip are two different people, Serenity."

"They are," she acknowledged, "but Phillip would grow to resent me, also. Especially if he believes, like Larry, that I'm supposed to be behind the pulpit instead of hosting what some consider to be nothing more than a talk show."

"Get up. I want you to go somewhere with me," her mother said, rising out of her chair.

"I've got a lot of work to get done, Mom. I really don't have time to go anywhere."

"When I walked into your office, you were resting your head on the desk and crying. You're in no condition to work. So, get your coat, and let's go."

"Where are we going?"

"Just put your coat on and do what your mother says." Clearly, she wasn't about to take no for an answer.

Reluctantly, Serenity grabbed her coat and followed her mother to her car. When they pulled into the parking lot at Abundant Life Christian Church, she wanted to lock her door and declare that she wasn't getting out. But her mother gave her one of those stares, as if she were a defiant six-year-old, so she opened her door and got out of the car. "I have no clue why you brought me here," she muttered.

Serenity trailed her mother into the church and toward the pastoral office suite. Pastor Matthew was seated at his desk when they walked into his office. He stood up, came around from behind his desk, and gave Serenity's mother a hug. When he turned to embrace Serenity, she stiffened and offered a lukewarm pat in return. "So, what brings you lovely ladies to my side of town?" he asked.

"We came for answers, Pastor Matthew, and I hope you have time to give them to us," Serenity's mother said.

"Anything for you. Have a seat," he said, pointing to the brown, leather couch to the left of his desk. He then sat down in the overstuffed chair next to the couch. "What's this all about?"

When they were seated, Serenity's mother began, "I'd like for you to explain to Serenity why you decided to leave our ministry, and why certain members ended up at your church."

"That happened twenty years ago, Lady Evelyn. You want to rehash it all now?" Pastor Matthew asked, clearly puzzled.

"What's wrong, Pastor?" Serenity spoke up. "Does it hurt to remember how you stole my father's members and mistreated a man who was nothing but kind and generous toward you?"

"Serenity," her mother admonished her.

"No, Mom. You're right—I think it's high time that Pastor Matthew answer for his sins."

Her mother turned to Pastor Matthew. "Please, tell her the truth, and don't leave anything out."

Pastor Matthew leaned back in his seat for a moment. He looked from her mother to her, then back again. "You never told her what happened?"

"I never knew she was harboring resentment toward you until she grew up. By that point, Lawrence thought she'd figure things out eventually, so he thought we should just leave it alone."

"I heard you arguing with my father," Serenity said. "I was twelve years old, but I knew that you had upset him. Then, he started moping around the house and the church. He didn't seem to be happy at all. And then, one day, he up and announced to the church that you were leaving to start your own ministry. You stabbed him in the back."

"Is that the way you saw it?" Pastor Matthew asked her.

"That's the way it happened," she shot back.

"Okay, I'm going to tell you a few things about myself and your father, who is my mentor to this day. Your father has always been like a big brother to me, and I would never intentionally do anything to hurt him."

Serenity didn't respond but kept a scowl of skepticism on her face.

"I started my first church when I was twenty-seven," he went on. "I was young and on fire for the Lord. But I didn't know the first thing about running a ministry. I had about fifty members, and ten of them were related to me. I met your father as I was entering my second year of ministry. He'd started his ministry about the same time that I had, but he had about six hundred members, and his ministry was doing great things for the Lord. Lawrence told me that if I joined forces with him, he would show me how to build my ministry so that I could accomplish all that God had for me.

"I didn't hesitate. I went back to my little storefront church and told the members that I was joining New Hope, where Pastor Lawrence Williams presided, and I invited them to join me there. Just about all of my members came over to New Hope, and we helped build Lawrence's church as if it were our own. Ten years went by, and New Hope grew to over five thousand members. That's when God started preparing my heart to leave."

"Don't stop there," Serenity's mother pressed Pastor Matthew. "Tell her all of it."

"I'm not sure if she needs to hear all of this," Pastor Matthew said quietly.

"Please, Pastor Matthew. Serenity is destroying her own happiness over a misunderstanding that arose from not hearing it," her mother said.

He nodded and then turned back to Serenity. "The argument you heard me having with your father had to do with my leaving—you're right about that, Serenity. But you're wrong about the circumstances.

"See, your father had promised that he would help me get my ministry off the ground if I would help him build his. At the time, I had no idea how I could help him, since I couldn't even get more than fifty people to show up on a Sunday morning. But your father saw something in me that I hadn't even seen in myself. I'm very organized, so I was able to help your father set up and maintain various ministries within the church, which have proven very useful for the work of the ministry.

"I guess your father just wasn't prepared to lose me, even if it was God's time for me to go. He was upset and tried to force me to stay. I told him that I couldn't. Even though I didn't want to leave his ministry, I knew God was calling me to my own."

"Are you trying to tell me that my father was holding you back from something God had called you to do?" Serenity asked.

Pastor Matthew didn't answer the question directly. Instead, he just said, "I needed money to begin my ministry. Your father had promised to loan me the necessary financing, but when it was time for me to go, he refused."

"My father has never gone back on his word in his life," Serenity said, coming to her father's defense. She looked at her mother. "Tell him, Mom. Daddy must've had a reason for not giving him the money."

Her mother put a hand on Serenity's shoulder and said, "Pastor Matthew is telling you the truth, Serenity. Please, just listen."

Pastor Matthew continued. "I knew that your father was having a hard time dealing with the fact that I would soon be leaving New Hope, so I stopped asking for his help. I found this broken-down, old building, which my wife and I put our pennies together to buy, and we spent a year working on that building, trying to bring it up to code. Then, one day, your father called me to his office and apologized. He said that God had shown him how selfish he was being, and that he wanted to make it up to me."

"Is that when he made the announcement about your new church?"

"Yes. But he did something else, too—he paid several contractors to make all the repairs on that dilapidated building we had bought, and he sent your mother to help Margie decorate the entire place. When they finished, Abundant Life looked so much better than we'd ever dreamed it would. When we were ready to move out of our temporary storefront, I was able to put the down payment on this building because of how much that first building sold for."

"Okay, then, can you tell me why so many of Daddy's members left his church and started attending yours, instead?" Serenity asked.

"First of all, your father and I were never of the mind that the members of a church 'belong' to one pastor or another. They belong to God, and He moves them where He sees fit. But, to answer your question, I believe about two hundred or so of the people who had been attending New Hope left to join Abundant Life. Most of my original members came back to Abundant Life, and, by then, they had children and grandchildren, who came with them. A few additional people came with us, but it was not because I solicited the New Hope members. I would never do that."

"I don't want to keep you any longer so that you can get back to your work," Serenity's mother said, standing and shaking Pastor Matthew's hand. "Thanks for taking the time to speak with us."

"Evelyn, you know that there's nothing I wouldn't do for you and your family." Pastor Matthew stood, turned to Serenity, and asked, "So, are we okay?"

It took Serenity a moment to reply, but as she'd been processing everything she'd heard, she'd realized that she actually believed Pastor Matthew. She stood and gave him a hug, warm and genuine this time. "We are more than okay, Pastor Matthew. Thank you for being honest with me. And I am so sorry for the way I spoke to you when we first arrived. Please forgive me."

Twenty-two

SERENITY HAD A LOT TO THINK ABOUT. SHE HAD MADE many life decisions based on a big misunderstanding. Michael had called off their engagement partly because he'd been jealous, but also because she'd been lukewarm about supporting him in his ministry. Phillip wanted to be with her, but she'd sent him away because she'd wanted nothing to do with his ministry, either; and it was based mainly on a misperception of something that had happened to her father.

"Why didn't Daddy tell me the truth years ago?" Serenity asked her mother as they drove back to the studio.

"He wanted to, honey, but I think he was worried that you would think less of him."

"I could never think less of Daddy. It might have taken him a while to come around, but he did help Pastor Matthew."

"The thing to remember is that without your dad's help, Pastor Matthew might still be in a storefront. But you also need to understand that, without Pastor Matthew's help, your dad might never have become a bishop with multiple churches in his fellowship. Pastor Matthew helped organize New Hope to the point where your dad was able to take on other responsibilities. So, God put them in each other's lives to help fulfill His purposes for them, and neither one of them has forgotten that, even if things did get a little out of hand there for some time."

"Now I feel bad, because I've blamed Pastor Matthew for something that I didn't understand completely."

"My mother always told me that erasers were put on pencils so that we could clean up our mistakes," Serenity's mother said.

"Yeah, well, my mother told me the same thing," Serenity said as they rounded the bend approaching her studio. When they were one block from their destination, she told her mother to pull over.

"What's wrong?" her mother asked as she pulled up alongside the curb.

"There's someone walking around my car. I'm calling the police," Serenity said, then opened her cell phone and dialed 9-1-1. When the operator answered, she gave the address of her studio and told the operator that it looked like someone was about to vandalize her car again.

When Serenity hung up, her mother said, "What's he doing?!"

Serenity looked and saw that the person kneeling next to her car was wearing a baseball hat and a bomber jacket. She didn't think that she was looking at a man, though. "That's a woman, Mom."

"No way—look at how he's slashing your tire! No woman I know has that kind of strength."

When the person moved on to the next tire, Serenity wanted to jump out of the car and confront him or her. But then, she imagined her chest being slashed, instead, and she decided to stay in her seat. "What's taking the police so long?"

"You just called them. Relax. They'll be here."

"But she's going to get away!"

"Oh, no, he's not! If I have to hit him with my car to buy some time for the police to get here, then that's what I'll do."

"I'm telling you, Mom, that's not a he."

A police car pulled in front of the studio just as the slasher stood up, dropped the knife, and tried to run. The police officer was quick, as if he'd expected to be dealing with a sprinter. He jumped out of his car, ran up the street after the slasher, and then made a tackle on the sidewalk right in front of Serenity and her mother, who cheered.

As the police officer handcuffed the slasher, Serenity watched in stunned silence as the hat fell off the woman's head and the police officer turned her around. She was staring at Michael's girlfriend, Karen.

⤨

"I want to speak with her," Serenity told Detective Roundtree. She had been at the police station for two hours, waiting patiently for Karen to be processed. In the meantime, she'd called Triple A and requested that they tow her car and replace another round of slashed tires. She was sleepy and tired and so irritated by the whole matter that she couldn't wait another second.

"I can't just let you in there. That woman might be in custody, but she still has rights."

"Can you ask if she'll agree to speak with me, please?"

Roundtree huffed a sigh. "Okay. Wait right here; I'll be back in a few," he said.

"Are you sure you want to do this?" Serenity's mother asked her.

"I've never done anything to this woman. I need to know why she did this to me."

Roundtree came back into the waiting room. "Follow me," he said.

Serenity followed him to the visiting area, where Karen was already seated at a table with her hands cuffed.

She sat down across from her and studied her for a moment before asking, "I've met you only once, right?"

"At the Mexican restaurant, yeah. So?" Karen said as she rolled her eyes.

"What I'm getting at is, I don't know you. So, I don't understand why you slit my tires."

Karen didn't respond.

"Did you also send that e-mail to me the first day I interviewed Phillip McKnight on my show?"

"Michael called you, and I wanted you to stay away from him."

"Michael called me that day because he was trying to get an interview. He wasn't trying to get back with me or anything."

"That's what you think."

"Nothing is going on between Michael and me. He wants to marry you—he told me so, himself."

"Then, where's my ring? Because I certainly haven't received it."

"Maybe he hasn't purchased it yet. I don't know. But none of that is my business. I just want to know why you slit my tires."

"I wasn't trying to hurt you," Karen said, rolling her eyes again. "The first time, I was going to drive by when you were stranded and pick you up so that we could talk. But Phillip McKnight was with you, so I didn't get a chance to talk to you because you left with him. Since I knew he'd gone back to Tampa, I figured I could get your attention tonight."

"Why didn't you just simply come into the studio and ask to speak to me?" Serenity asked, still not understanding this woman's thinking.

"Yeah, right. Ask Ms. Look-but-Don't-Touch for a moment of her time? You would have had one of your security guards throw me out."

Serenity didn't have security guards—some of the cameramen performed in that capacity, as needed. But she wasn't about to tell that to Karen. Still, she was curious about Karen's impression of her.

Karen continued, "I used to watch your program all the time, and I found it uplifting. I believed that God was speaking to me through your messages. But, then, I met Michael and found out that you won't even take the time to shake the hands of people who travel hundreds of miles to hear you preach."

"That's not true," Serenity said, though her conviction was failing her.

"Yes, it is. I heard comments like that about you from other people even before I met Michael, but I never believed them. Then, some of Michael's church members told me that you barely ever spoke to them. You would wait in his office after the service so that you didn't have to talk to anyone. You're pathetic."

Serenity wanted to object to this stalker woman calling her pathetic, but she had to admit that there was some truth to her words. She'd thought that, by keeping her distance from the people she ministered to, she could keep herself safe from being hurt. But, if what Karen had said was to be believed, she had been hurting the people of God with her standoffish behavior.

She stood up and walked out of the visitation room without saying another word to Karen. Her heart was heavy with guilt as she approached her mother. "Let's get out of here," Serenity said.

When they were back in the car, her mother turned to her and said, "What did that woman say to you? I haven't seen this look on your face since your high school sweetheart took another girl to the prom."

"I got over that cheater within a week. But, this? I'm not so sure, Mom," Serenity said. She leaned back against the headrest and sighed.

"What happened?"

"She said that I'm a look-but-don't-touch type of person, and that I don't care about the people I minister to because I won't even take time to speak to them. She called me pathetic."

"Oh, Serenity. You are not pathetic. Please don't take what that woman said to heart."

"How can I not take it to heart? She might be a stalker, but she's right. I don't want to be bothered with people. Look at the way I treated Pastor Matthew when I didn't have the whole story."

Her mother sighed, then started the car. As she pulled out of the parking lot, she said, "You're coming home with me tonight."

"No, Mom," Serenity protested. "I need to be alone tonight. I need to spend some time in prayer."

"I don't know if you should be alone right now, Serenity. You've been going through a lot lately. I think you need to be around your family."

Serenity put her hand on her mother's shoulder. "I know you're worried about me, Mom, but this is something I need to figure out on my own—with God's help."

"All right, honey. If you're sure," her mother said, pulling up next to Serenity's car at the garage where it had been towed.

"Triple A is going to cancel my membership if they have to tow my car one more time to get new tires."

"At least you were smart enough to join. I say, every single woman needs a Triple A membership."

Serenity leaned over and gave her mother a hug. "Thanks for everything you did for me tonight, Mom."

"Call me if you need me," her mother said.

"I will," Serenity said as she got out of the car. She opened her car door, got in, and drove home to face her demons.

Twenty-three

SERENITY TOOK A SHOWER, PUT ON HER PAJAMAS, AND then curled up on her bed with her Bible. She was numb from the events of the evening. Not only had she discovered that she'd been carrying around a grudge for something she never should have been angry about in the first place, but also, someone else was holding a grudge against her for something she hadn't done, either.

Karen's actions didn't make sense to her because she didn't think she'd given the woman any reason to believe that she wanted Michael back. And Michael had claimed that he wanted to marry Karen. It was just Karen's bad luck to meet a man as fickle as Michael Randolph. Still, Serenity had nothing to do with that. She would have understood if Karen had slit Michael's tires, but, no, she'd chosen to pick on her. Even as she wondered about Karen's motives, Serenity could hear Phillip saying, "Sometimes, things just happen, even when we've done nothing to prevent or provoke them."

Maybe Phillip was right. Maybe she needed to stop worrying about other people's motives and concentrate on her own. She bowed her head and prayed that God would give her direction as she searched through His Word. She wanted to figure out how she'd become so messed up. She wanted to change, but she needed God to open her eyes and guide her down the path He desired for her to take. She opened her Bible and went back to the same passage in the eighth chapter of the book of John that had given her pause a couple of months ago. Tonight, verses 31 and 32 particularly resonated with her: *"Then Jesus said to those Jews who believed him, 'If you abide in My word, you are My disciples indeed. And you shall know the truth, and the truth shall make you free.'"*

Serenity remembered thinking that God was trying to show her something in these verses when she'd studied them earlier, but she hadn't labored over their meaning. Now, she bowed her head in prayer and said, "Lord, please help me understand what You want me to know. This Scripture says that I need to abide in Your Word in order to be Your disciple. So, there must be something in this Bible that will help me with what I'm going through right now. Please direct me there."

Another Scripture came to mind, one she had memorized in Sunday school—Psalm 133:1: *"Behold, how good and how pleasant it is for brethren to dwell together in unity!"* Serenity knew that God wanted His people to be unified. She wanted the same thing; she just didn't know how she could be a part of that unity when she didn't trust the people of God and had been holding unforgiveness in her heart toward some of them since childhood.

Church members always seemed to think that being a preacher's kid was such a great thing. They also seemed to envy preachers' children's access to the men and women of God that was unavailable to them. But that access had also enabled Serenity to see Christians behaving in ungodly ways toward her mother and father. She had been hurt by what she'd witnessed, but she'd never in a million years imagined that her own actions would hurt others.

Her mother had said that Larry had been able to forgive Mark Sampson and move on after the schism in his church, but, for some reason, Serenity was stuck and didn't know how to get to the place where she needed to be. She desperately wanted to get there, though, so she flipped through the pages of her Bible, praying that God would open her heart to understand what she read. When she came to 2 Corinthians, one of her favorite of Paul's epistles, she started reading in chapter two, verse 4, and continued through verse 11:

> *For out of much affliction and anguish of heart I wrote unto you, with many tears, not that you should be grieved, but that you might know the love which I have so abundantly for you. But if anyone has caused grief, he has not grieved me, but all of you to some extent; not to be too severe. This punishment which was inflicted by the majority is sufficient for such a man, so that, on the contrary, you ought rather to forgive and comfort him, lest perhaps such a one be swallowed up with too much sorrow. Therefore I urge you to reaffirm your love to him. For to this end I also wrote, that I might put you to the test, whether you are obedient in all things. Now whom you forgive anything, I also forgive. For if indeed I have forgiven anything, I have forgiven that one for your sakes in the presence of Christ, lest Satan should take advantage of us; for we are not ignorant of his devices.*

In this letter, the apostle Paul wrote to the church at Corinth concerning some less than honorable behavior that some of its members had displayed. He asked them to forgive this person who had committed an offense within the church, especially so that Satan would not be able to take advantage of them.

Looking back, Serenity realized that even though she had been fighting against the works of evil all her life, she had allowed herself to be deceived. She had thought that it was okay to harbor unforgiveness against others because of what they'd done to her or to her family. But God was showing her that it was not.

Several months ago, she had read an article that had asked if the black church in America was dead or just lukewarm. Serenity had believed it was lukewarm, and now she realized why. If the other preachers in the black community were dealing with issues like she was, then how could any of them truly effect change in the people of God? Tears filled her eyes, and she lay down on her bed and cried. Curled up in a ball, she held her Bible close to her heart.

"I'm so sorry, Lord," she cried out. "I see now that my inability to forgive others has hindered not just my ministry, but also my growth as a Christian." She wanted to change, but since she'd seemed to always be worried about people betraying her, as Michael had done, she didn't know if she had it in her to forgive, forget, and move on. She fell asleep, still waiting on God to answer the question that troubled her heart.

When she awoke the next morning, Serenity had a pounding headache. She got up, went to the bathroom for two Tylenols, and then slowly walked back into her bedroom.

She noticed that her Bible was opened to the book of Proverbs. Since wisdom flowed from the book of Proverbs like water from the sea, she sat down on her bed, closed her eyes, and prayed for understanding before starting to read. She began in Proverbs 29, and she was struck by verse 25: *"The fear of man brings a snare, but whoever trusts in the LORD shall be safe."*

That was it! She didn't have to fear what man would, could, or might do. She was supposed to put her trust in the Lord, because it was God's job, not her own, to keep her safe. And, hadn't the Lord been keeping her safe all this time? She hadn't lost her mind when Michael had called off their wedding. She hadn't been alone when Karen had slashed her tires. And, when those hoodlums had ransacked her studio, God had kept her safe then, too. No one had been hurt, and so many people had chipped in to help fix up the studio. Phillip had been there for her when that had happened, as well, and yet all she'd done had been to blame him and his ex-wife for everything that was happening to her. None of it had been his fault.

She wanted to talk to Phillip, but she was so ashamed of the way she'd treated him. The man had professed his love for her, and she'd sent him away because of her own insecurities.

She wanted to talk to Phillip and tell him how much she appreciated everything he'd done for her. She had some other things to tell him, too, but, after the way she'd treated him, she was afraid that he wouldn't answer the phone when he saw her number. So, she took the chicken's way out—she sent him an e-mail.

After that, Serenity called her mother. When she picked up, Serenity said, "Hi, Mom. I need to shop. Would you like to join me?"

"You know I would. Let me fix your father's breakfast, and then I'll get dressed."

"Okay. I'll pick you up in about an hour."

Serenity hummed to herself as she ironed her outfit, took a shower, and got dressed.

As she was pulling out of her driveway, her cell phone rang. She looked at the caller ID and saw that it was Michael. "Hey, Michael," she said when she answered. "How are you doing?"

"Hi, Serenity. I just found out what Karen did, and I wanted to make sure that you knew that I had nothing to do with this."

"I don't blame you for Karen's actions, Michael. Please don't give it a second thought."

"So, we're okay? You're not mad at me anymore?"

"Michael, the truth is, I was mad at you for a long time. I'd lumped you in with all the other people I thought I had a right to be ticked off with. But that wasn't right, and I want you to know that I forgive you."

"I'm so glad to hear that, Serenity, because I made the biggest mistake of my life when I called off our wedding. I was hoping that we could talk about getting back together."

What?! "I don't know about that, Michael."

"I know we won't be like we used to be—at least, not right away. But, if we take it slow—a lunch here, a dinner there—you never know how things might turn out."

Serenity knew that Michael wasn't the man for her. She hadn't seen it in their five years of dating and being engaged, but she could see it clearly now. "We're not right for each other, Michael. I do hope you find that special someone, though."

"But *you* were special—you've always been special to me," Michael said, regret in his voice.

"I've got to go, Michael. I wish you well." With that, Serenity ended the call and pulled into her parents' driveway.

Seconds later, her mother came out the front door, walked down the driveway, and opened the door on the passenger side. "Hi, honey! Are you feeling better today?" she asked, easing herself into the seat.

"Hi, Mom. My time with the Lord helped more than you'll ever know. I see things so much more clearly this morning."

"I'm glad," her mother said as she buckled her seat belt.

"But, Mom, you also helped me. Thanks for letting me know the truth about Pastor Matthew. In a way, it's helping me to look for the good in others and not to assume the worst about them."

The two women hit their usual shopping spots, hunting for bargains and having a great time. In every store, Serenity took time to smile at other people who crossed her path. She had a conversation about fashion trends with a teenaged girl at one of the boutiques, and, at another, she talked with a clerk about the hottest colors of the season.

"What's gotten into you?" her mother asked as they loaded some of their bags into the trunk of the car.

"Nothing. I just realized that I need to take the time to get to know people. And the only way I'm going to do that is to open my mouth and talk to them." Receiving revelation from God was an awesome thing, but this particular revelation had set Serenity free from fearing people, and she never planned to be a captive to fear again. As a matter of fact, she felt like dancing as they entered the next boutique. There were tons of shoppers in the store, and Serenity planned to speak to them all.

Twenty-four

PHILLIP WAS PUTTING THE FINISHING TOUCHES ON HIS sermon when he noticed that he'd received a new e-mail. When he saw that it was from Serenity, he froze for a second. He wasn't sure that he wanted to open it. He was trying to come to terms with the fact that he and Serenity were not going to be together, and he didn't want to read her message and find himself wishing and dreaming that things could be different.

Serenity didn't want the same things he wanted; worse, she didn't want *him*. He moved his cursor over to the delete button and clicked, then went back to his sermon, reading it once more to make sure he hadn't left out anything. When he was satisfied with the sermon, he started to shut down his computer, but curiosity got the better of him. He reopened his e-mail account, clicked on his deleted items folder, opened her e-mail, and started to read.

Phillip,

It's been only a week or so since you left, and yet I've gone through so many emotions and figured out so much since then that it seems like you've been gone a lot longer.

I found out who slit my tires, and you were right—Chantel had nothing to do with it. Michael's girlfriend, Karen, was responsible all along. I'm sorry I didn't believe you.

You probably don't want to hear from me right now, but I'm so sorry that I asked you to leave. I didn't mean it, and, now, I don't know how to take any of it back. Anyway, I just wanted you to know that I miss you. I'm signing off of my computer now, because I feel like shopping.

Love,
Serenity

Like a teenager with his first crush, Phillip reread Serenity's e-mail three more times, practically memorizing it. Did this mean what he thought? Was she finally ready to give him a chance? He wasn't going to sit there all day wondering. He searched online for flight schedules and found one for Chicago at 11:00 a.m. Since Chicago was one hour behind Tampa, he figured he could get there and have a rental car before one in the afternoon. He showered and changed into a pair of jeans and a sweatshirt before grabbing his keys and heading out the door.

When Phillip was halfway to the airport, Derek called him. "What's up, Derek?" he asked.

"Hey, man! Some of the fellas and I were trying to get a game going today, and I wanted to know if you were interested in being the quarterback," Derek said.

"Last time I was quarterback, it was a disaster. What's going on? Are you feeling sorry for me or something?"

"Yeah, I know you were a bit down in the dumps last night, so I thought a game might cheer you up."

"Well, I'll have to take a rain check. I'm on my way back to Chicago."

"I thought you said that was over," Derek reminded him.

"Serenity e-mailed me this morning, and I think she's ready to give us a chance. Anyway, I've got to give this one more shot."

"You never were a throw-in-the-towel type of player; that's what made you great on the field. But I don't know about this one, man," Derek said.

"I've got to give it a shot, Derek. She's the one for me. I can't stop thinking about her."

"Okay, but you do know that I'm telling the guys about how lovesick you are, right?"

"Tell them anything you want," Phillip said. "When I come back with my woman, we'll see who gets the last laugh."

⁓

"Oh, Serenity, this shirt is perfect for you," her mother said, pulling a purple blouse off the rack.

"You want me to try it on?" Serenity took the garment and headed toward the dressing rooms.

She was intercepted by a woman dressed in jeans and a T-shirt printed with the words, "Jesus Is My Everything." "Hey! Aren't you Serenity Williams?" she said with a grin.

"Yes, I am. What's your name?" Serenity asked, not missing the look of shock on her mother's face as she looked through a bin of sunglasses behind the woman. Normally, when someone recognized her, Serenity would simply confirm her identity and then walk away as fast as she could. But this was a new day.

"My name is Vicki Reese, and I watch your program every chance I get. I was watching the day you called Pastor McKnight gorgeous. And, if you don't mind my saying so, you were right," she said with a wink.

Serenity laughed. "I received a lot of grief about that slip. But, the truth is, the man is not only gorgeous; he's also the most humble man I've ever met, and I don't think he even realizes how handsome he is."

"Somebody needs to give that man a mirror," Vicki said with a laugh, and Serenity smiled. This was big—she was having a friendly conversation with a woman who wasn't Melinda or her mother.

They conversed for a little longer, and then Serenity held up the purple blouse. "I'm supposed to try this on, so I guess I'd better get going. Thanks for watching *Walk This Way*, Vicki. I really appreciate it."

"Just keep doing what you're doing. I've been growing spiritually since I started watching your show, so I'll be a viewer for life," Vicki said before walking away.

Inside the dressing room, Serenity sat down on the chair, bowed her head, and silently thanked the Lord for enabling her to trust Him enough to take the initiative to reach out to others. Vicki had told her that she'd been growing spiritually because of her show. If Serenity had just brushed her off, as she had done to so many other people, would Vicki have stopped growing closer to the Lord because of her actions?

Serenity couldn't afford to forget that Karen had long been a viewer of her program, too, and she had been turned off because of some things she'd heard about her, such as how standoffish and cold she was. If Serenity could have taken it all back, she would have. But, life was funny. You had to lie in the bed you made.

A knock on the dressing room door brought her out of her musings.

"Are you still in there?" her mother called.

"Yeah, but I haven't tried on the shirt yet. I was just thinking," Serenity admitted.

"Well, I've got a few more things for you to try," her mother said.

Serenity opened the door and gawked at the pile of clothes draped over her mother's arm. "Mom, I'll be in here all day if I try on all those outfits."

"Do you have anything better to do today?" her mother asked, thrusting the clothes at her.

"Okay, fine," Serenity relented. "I'll try them on."

"Great," her mother said as she handed off the clothes. "Make sure you come out and let me see how each one looks."

⌒

Phillip had been to five of the best consignment shops in the city of Chicago and still hadn't found Serenity. The store clerks at three of the shops knew her and confirmed that she had shopped there earlier that day. He was about to give up and go to her condo to wait for her to come home when he decided to call Bishop Williams, instead. Derek was already laughing at him, and so he was trying to keep his humiliation to a minimum. However, Phillip really thought that Bishop Williams was rooting for him. Surely, he wouldn't mind helping him track down his daughter.

He dialed the Williams' number and, when Bishop Williams picked up, shamelessly confessed, "I'm looking for Serenity, Bishop. I've been to five different consignment shops this afternoon but haven't been able to find her."

"Boy, you must be in love," Bishop Williams said, chuckling. "I used to track Evelyn on her shopping expeditions, and, let me tell you—that was hard. Lucky for you, I happen to know that she's at the mall."

"Thank goodness! I thought I'd never find her."

"Hold on while I call Evelyn to find out which store they're in. That mall is like a maze, you know." After a few minutes' pause, Phillip heard Bishop Williams say, "Phillip? You still there? I found them! They're in Macy's."

When Phillip had received general directions to get him there, he said, "Thank you, sir. I appreciate your help."

"Yeah, well, just don't mess it up this time. I'd like to be able to call you son sometime soon," Bishop Williams said with a laugh.

If Serenity's e-mail meant what Phillip thought it did, he wasn't worried about messing anything up. He just needed to get to her, because he was almost at the point where he couldn't move another muscle. How she and her mother managed these all-day shopping sprees was beyond him. It took him thirty minutes to get from the consignment shop to the mall. After he parked his car, he called Lady Evelyn's cell phone. "I'm finally here, Lady Evelyn. Are you still in Macy's?"

"Yep, but you'd better hurry up. I've just given her three more outfits to try on, and she's getting antsy."

"I'm on my way. Please, don't leave—I've been tracking you and Serenity all day, and I'm about to pass out."

"Lawrence could never keep up with me, either," Lady Evelyn said with a laugh. "See you soon!"

Phillip was glad he'd let Derek talk him into putting a fitness center in the church. He needed to stay in shape just to keep up with Serenity's shopping. He ran into the mall through the main entrance and hurried toward

Macy's. On the way, he passed JCPenney, New York & Company, and several other stores, and when he rounded the corner and found himself staring at the Macy's sign, he had to stop and catch his breath.

Trying to look cool and composed, he walked into Macy's and found the ladies' department where they were. Lady Evelyn was standing by a rack of dresses near the dressing rooms, and he approached her and tapped her on the shoulder.

"About time you got here!" she exclaimed, giving him a hug. "I was worried that I'd have to tell her what was going on."

"I'm glad you didn't—I want to surprise her," Phillip said.

Just then, the dressing room door opened, and Serenity emerged. She was looking down at her dress as she walked, trying to adjust it. "I hope you like this one, Mom, because it's the last thing I'm going to try on."

"It's beautiful," Phillip said, gazing steadily at Serenity.

Serenity jerked her head up and stopped in her tracks, then stood there in shocked silence for what seemed like a minute.

"I just want to know if you meant it," he went on.

With a look of confusion, Serenity asked, "Meant what?"

He walked toward her. "You signed your e-mail, 'Love, Serenity.' So, I came here to find out if you meant it." He touched her cheek. "Do you really love me, Serenity?"

She opened her mouth, as if to answer, but tears were flowing down her face, and she couldn't get a word out.

"I'm not leaving until you tell me," he said gently.

Serenity leaned her head on Phillip's shoulder as she wiped the tears from her face. When she had calmed down, she lifted her face and smiled. "Yes, Phillip. I love you."

He lowered his head and kissed her, long and tenderly. When they parted, he said, "What took you so long? I've loved you since the day we met."

Epilogue

F IVE MONTHS LATER, ON A FRIDAY MORNING, SERENITY was on the set of her show with her three guests: Melinda Marks and two other women who, like Serenity and Melinda, were preachers' kids. Cindy Marlow had started an organization to help adults celebrate and recover from issues they'd faced while growing up in the home of a preacher parent, and Darlene was an evangelist and a recovering addict who had ended up on drugs while trying to run from the call of God on her life. After seeing all that her parents endured, she hadn't wanted anything to do with the ministry. Darlene's story of survival had helped bring thousands into the kingdom of God.

Being a preacher's kid came with more hardships than most people realized, and the four women were going to discuss the issue live on *Walk This Way*. When the camera cut to Serenity and started rolling, she said, "Welcome, and thank you for joining me for *Walk This Way*. Today, I'd like to open up about an issue that I've been dealing with all my life, and I have some friends here who have dealt with the same issue." After introducing Melinda, Cindy, and Darlene, she said, "The four of us are preachers' kids, and, today, we're going to talk about the joys and pains of being part of a ministry-minded family."

For Serenity, a program on this topic was long over-due. She sat with the women and openly discussed issues that she would have guarded with her life a few months ago. Now, she was exposing herself to her viewers in the hopes that her struggles would help some of them—es-pecially those with a parent in the ministry—release un-forgiveness and move past the painful experiences they might have endured.

Cindy spoke about the types of issues some of the preachers' kids within her organization have dealt with. Then, Serenity admitted that her own issues had been so severe that she'd been against the idea not only of be-coming a preacher, but also of marrying one, because she didn't want to deal with a congregation; she didn't want to worry about the damage her husband's parishioners might do to her children.

Halfway through the segment, Serenity saw Phillip walk in and take a seat in the audience. He looked so hand-some in his navy blue suit with a baby blue silk tie, and she couldn't help her girlish grin. She and Phillip were an official couple, and this was his weekend to visit her.

Melinda discussed how difficult it had been for her to earn respect as a preacher in her own right, since she'd stayed in her father's fellowship and had his shadow to contend with. Darlene told stories about living on the streets and begging for money, which she would use to get high, until her father found her and begged her to come back home.

It was an emotional show for Serenity, her guests, and many members of the studio audience, judging by the sniffles and sobs that could be heard. Serenity was touched to think how this program must be hitting home with a lot of her viewers, and she silently thanked God for helping her to get over her problems and to open up about them with candor so that others might find help in dealing with similar issues.

When the clock showed ten minutes left in the program, Serenity heard Pam's voice in her earbud: "Excuse me, Serenity, but someone in the audience has a question."

She wondered why Pam was asking her to field a question right now, especially since they'd planned an extra question-and-answer program to immediately follow this one. She figured Pam had some reason, though.

So, after her assistant, Sandy, brought a microphone stand down the aisle and set it up near the stage, Serenity said, "Someone out there has a question, so come on down to the microphone and ask away."

The next thing she knew, Phillip was standing up and making his way toward the front as heads turned and women in the audience murmured to one another. He tapped the microphone and then said, "I'm sorry to interrupt, but I have an important question."

What was going on here? The segment was almost over; why wouldn't Phillip just wait and ask his question along with everybody else in the next segment? She glanced over at Melinda, but her friend just smiled and shrugged her shoulders. Serenity then looked out at Phillip. "What's your question?"

"I just want to know if you've gotten over your fear of marrying a preacher."

Serenity dropped her jaw. His question caught her completely off guard, and she didn't know how she should respond, especially with so many people watching.

While she was still trying to figure out what to say, Phillip stepped away from the microphone and started walking toward the stage. He climbed the stairs, got down on one knee beside Serenity, and said, "Serenity Williams, would you make this preacher a happy man?"

She leaned closer to him and whispered, "What are you doing, Phillip? We're on television!"

"I don't care," he said, pulling a small box out of his coat pocket. When he opened the box and held it up to her, Serenity almost fainted at the sight of the beautiful, five-carat, emerald-cut diamond ring. "Marry me, Serenity. I need you in my life."

Months ago, when Phillip had told her that he wanted to be in her life and had asked if she wanted to be in his life, she'd ignored the question because she'd been afraid of what that would entail. Since then, she had done a lot of praying and soul-searching. Serenity wasn't afraid anymore. She would willingly stand by Phillip's side for the rest of her life; she would partner with him in ministry, even as she continued with her own show as long as that was feasible, and help fulfill his God-given visions in any way she could. She was now ready to be all that God had intended her to be, including a wife to this wonderful preacher man, with whom she was madly in love. "Yes, Phillip," she finally said, trying to remain calm. "I will marry you."

He jumped to his feet, picked her up, and swung her around as the audience cheered. Then, he whispered in her ear, "You know this means our children will be preacher's kids."

"And they will be blessed to have you as a father," Serenity added with joy in her heart. "Thank you, Phillip. Thank you for not giving up on me."

Discussion Questions

1. Serenity was called by God to minister, but, be-
    cause of past hurts, she was comfortable minis-
    tering only from a distance. Has something or
    someone ever hurt you so much that it stifled
    your ministry or your walk with God?

2. After Serenity's breakup with her fiancé, the Rev-
    erend Michael Randolph, she adopted the
    belief that most, if not all, male preachers
    were full of pride and driven by their egos.
    Because of his ex-wife's money lust, Phillip
    stayed away from women he perceived to be
    "high maintenance." Phillip and Serenity almost
    lost each other because of what someone else
    had done to them. Have you ever made make oth-
    ers pay for the mistakes of someone else?

3. Serenity had trust issues. She didn't like to get
    too close to people in the church because she
    assumed that she would eventually get hurt. She
    even worried that Phillip's friend, Elder Derek
    Mann, would try to steal Phillip's ministry. Where
    did her trust issues stem from? Do you have
    similar issues?

4. Do you believe it's better to trust but verify, as Serenity believed, or are you willing to trust God when you associate with other people?

5. In chapter three, Serenity reads John 8:32: *"And you shall know the truth, and the truth shall make you free."* Later on, Serenity realizes that Pastor Daniel Matthew was not the deceptive man she believed him to be, and this knowledge changes her view on people in the ministry and allows her to trust again. Have you ever had a similar experience of acquiring knowledge that altered your perspective in a healthy way?

6. Michael Randolph's prideful issues sent him into the arms of an insecure and vindictive woman. What has pride caused you to do that you wish you hadn't?

7. Phillip McKnight was a humble, God-fearing man, but he had trouble forgiving his ex-wife, Chantel. Do you think it was important for Phillip to forgive Chantel before pursuing a relationship with Serenity? If so, why?

About the Author

V anessa Miller of Dayton, Ohio, is a best-selling author, playwright, and motivational speaker. Her stage productions include *Get You Some Business, Don't Turn Your Back on God*, and *Can't You Hear Them Crying*. Vanessa is currently in the process of writing stage productions from her novels in the Rain series.

Vanessa has been writing since she was a young child. When she wasn't writing poetry, short stories, stage plays, and novels, reading great books consumed her free time. However, it wasn't until she committed her life to the Lord in 1994 that she realized all gifts and anointing come from God. She then set out to write redemption stories that glorified God.

Second Chance at Love is Vanessa's first series to be published by Whitaker House. Book one in the series, *Yesterday's Promise*, was number one on the Black Christian Book Club national bestsellers list in April 2010. In addition, Vanessa has published two other series, Forsaken and Rain, as well as a stand-alone title, *Long Time Coming*. Her books have received positive reviews, won Best Christian Fiction Awards, and topped best-sellers lists, including *Essence*. Vanessa is the recipient of numerous awards, including the Best Christian Fiction Mahogany Award 2003 and the Red Rose Award for Excellence in

Christian Fiction 2004, and she was nominated for the NAACP Image Award (Christian Fiction) 2004.

Vanessa is a dedicated Christian and devoted mother. She graduated from Capital University in Columbus, Ohio, with a degree in organizational communication. In 2007, Vanessa was ordained by her church as an exhorter. Vanessa believes this was the right position for her because God has called her to exhort readers and to help them rediscover their places with the Lord.

A preview of

A Promise of Forever Love

Book Three in the Second Chance at Love Series
by Vanessa Miller

Prologue

O N DAYS LIKE THIS, YVONNE MILNER WONDERED why she even bothered to pray. She had yelled, screamed, begged, and cajoled, yet the doctors still couldn't make eye contact with her when they came into her husband's hospital room. There were no more talks of surgery or chemotherapy. They'd told her that nothing more could be done for David. But, as far as Yvonne was concerned, the doctors didn't know diddly. David Milner was the senior pastor of one of the most notable churches in Detroit. He was the father of two beautiful daughters, and he was her beloved husband. So, she wasn't just going to throw in the towel and believe the doctors' doom-and-gloom predictions. She and David had been married for thirty-four years, and he had promised her a fiftieth wedding anniversary celebration. "We've got sixteen more years to go, David," she urged him. "Don't give up now."

A vicious cough shook his fragile, cancer-racked body as he attempted to sit up in his hospital bed.

"Don't, sweetheart. Just lie down."

"No...I need...to tell you...something." David labored to get each word out.

It was killing Yvonne to see her husband weak and bedridden like this. He had always been so strong, had always been her hero. She had admired this man, even when they hadn't seen eye-to-eye about her role in the ministry. Early in their marriage, Yvonne had known that she was destined to preach the gospel. However, David wouldn't hear of it. They had fought, and Yvonne had prayed for years that God would change her husband's mind. Finally, David had accepted the fact that his wife had been called by God to be a preacher. Yet, even through those tough years, Yvonne couldn't have imagined being anywhere else but with the man she loved. "You can say what you need to while lying down, honey. You need your strength to get better."

David shook his head. "I'm going home, baby."

"I know that, David. You just need to regain your strength so they will let you out of this hospital."

He shook his head again and then pointed heavenward. "Home…with Jesus."

Yvonne's eyes filled with tears. "Don't say that, David. You and I have a lot more living to do."

He patted her hand. "Call Thomas."

Thomas Reed was David's best friend. The man traveled the world building churches and ministering to God's people. He'd recently lost his wife to the same evil disease that was threatening to take David's life. "Call Thomas right now? Why? What do you want me to tell him?"

"If you need help, call Thomas. He promised me—" A coughing fit cut him off.

Yvonne took the cup from David's bedside table and filled it with water from the pitcher, then held the glass to his lips for him to drink once the coughing subsided. "Here, baby, drink this." When he had taken a few sips, she said, "Now, just lie here and rest. Our girls will be

here soon, and you need to save your energy for them."
Toya, twenty-nine years old, was their firstborn, a self-assured attorney with political aspirations. Tia was their twenty-six-year-old "baby." Whereas Toya was analytical and ambitious, Tia's strength was creativity, yet she was introspective and reserved. She could paint and write poetry from sunup till sundown and be perfectly at peace.

It had been difficult for Yvonne to manage her daughters' very different personalities while raising them, but David had convinced her to relax and let God work out His perfect plan for each girl's life. If it hadn't been for David's wisdom and prayers, Yvonne was sure that she would have broken Tia's spirit. She had needed more time than David to understand their daughter's passion for writing and painting. What was she going to do if he didn't survive this illness?

No sooner had the thought crossed her mind than Yvonne tried to banish it. But that was also the moment when she noticed that David's breathing sounded funny. And then she understood why none of the medical professionals who had come into the room today had been able to look her in the eye. They had heard it, too—the death rattle.

"No, baby, no—don't leave me!" she begged him.

"Remember...Thomas promised...love you."

Tears were running down Yvonne's face as she heard her husband's last words. She put her arms around the man she had loved for a lifetime—and yet not long enough—and whispered, "I love you, too, baby. Always and forever."

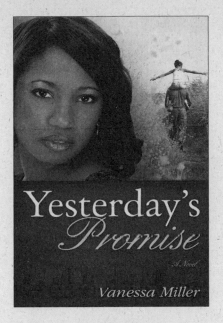

Yesterday's Promise
Vanessa Miller

Melinda Johnson has always felt called to ministry. So, when her father, Bishop Langston Johnson, decides to step down after thirty years, it seems only natural for her to take his place. But Bishop Johnson feels led by a God who has other things in mind, and to succeed him, he appoints Steven Marks—a man who is opposed to female pastors, not to mention the fact that he is Melinda's ex-fiancé. Can Steven and Melinda set aside past pains, forgive each other, and learn to love again? Or will their opposing positions regarding women preachers keep them forever at odds?

ISBN: 978-1-60374-207-8 ◆ Trade ◆ 240 pages

WHITAKER
HOUSE

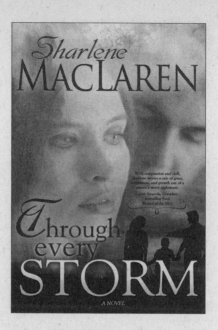

Through Every Storm
Sharlene MacLaren

Struggling through the tragic loss of their child, Maddie and Jeff Bowman experience the immense pain and grief caused by a broken heart and a marriage so severely strained that a divorce seems imminent. Will life ever be normal again? While still overwhelmed with feelings of complete hopelessness and loneliness, they are additionally faced with having to care for a precocious little boy. Maddie and Jeff must learn how to overcome their problems. But together they may find a joy and happiness that they had never known before.

ISBN: 978-0-88368-746-8 ✦ Trade ✦ 368 pages

WHITAKER
HOUSE

Tender Vow
Sharlene MacLaren

Whopen Jason Evans' brother, John, is killed in a skiing accident, Jason tries to soothe his guilt and grief by reaching out to his widowed sister-in-law, Rachel. He helps with her children, does odd jobs around her house, and tries to bolster her faith in the fog of pain and confusion.

Rachel, however, asserts her independence and resists being her brother-in-law's charity case, particularly since they have a history she'd rather forget. Soon, though, she finds that God has other plans for her—and for Jason. Can she accept the Lord's leading and still honor her late husband's memory?

ISBN: 978-1-60374-098-2 ♦ Trade ♦ 400 pages

WHITAKER
HOUSE

Long Journey Home
Sharlene MacLaren

Single mother Callie May is still nursing emotional scars from an abusive marriage when a handsome but brooding stranger moves into the apartment across the hall. In spite of his attractiveness, pastor Dan Mattson has problems of his own—he abandoned his flock and turned his back on God following the deaths of his wife and baby daughter. When Callie's ex-husband shows up to wreak even more havoc in her life, Dan comes to her defense—and faces his own demons in the process. Will Dan and Callie allow God to change their hearts and mend their hurts so they can take another chance on love?

ISBN: 978-1-60374-056-2 ◆ Trade ◆ 400 pages

WHITAKER
HOUSE